Every Single Wildflower

S.J. Chaynie

Cover design by S.J. Chaynie.

For the girls who just want a ruggedly handsome man with a cowboy hat, a smirk, and a deep southern drawl to call her darlin. This one's for you.

Contents

Blurb

Returning home to Mayson Ridge was the last thing I had planned. But after receiving an unexpected text reading *you need to come home,* and with no other reasonable excuse besides my own guilt, I had no other choice. I knew at some point I'd have to face my family, and being back in Mayson Ridge meant I'd unfortunately end up facing the man who shattered my heart before I left for good. I thought I'd see him in passing, a simple glance from across a crowded room. What I didn't expect was to find Maddox Sheppard working on my family ranch. Just like I didn't expect to be forced into teaming up with him to save what's left of the Mayson Ranch legacy. But old feelings still linger, the heartbreak fresh, and so many unspoken words between me and the rugged cowboy who secretly owns my heart. I'd have given it to him years ago...but he, along with the rest of this town thought it belonged to someone else. *To his brother.*

Prologue

Ivy

Seven years ago

I punch the green icon for the fourth time in a row, letting the line ring until my soon to be ex boyfriend's voice comes through the speaker with the voicemail greeting that I've been getting more often than not for the last four years.

"Sup. It's Brady, leave one."

With gritted teeth I glance at the empty parking lot of the Mayson Jar, my aunt's restaurant that has been closed for over an hour now. She was shorthanded this evening, so I worked a shift, and was supposed to be picked up by Brady when we closed at ten. But here I am, freezing my ass off, because as luck would have it, it's those rare two weeks that Texas actually has a winter. My eyes roll in annoyance, my anger flaring as I'm obviously forgotten, yet again.

It's your own fault, Ivy. Put your big girl pants on and end it.

I know I should have months ago. We'd been friends since kindergarten. He was my first kiss. My first boyfriend, and as much as I love Brady, I'm not in love with him. I would have had the hard conversation a couple of years ago, but when his dad died suddenly in a horrible accident, I couldn't bring myself to do it. He needed me during his grief, so I set aside my concerns and was there for him. But now.... it's becoming plain bullshit.

The vacant parking lot only reminds me that everyone is gone for the night, and I now need to find someone to drop their Friday night plans to accommodate my lack of backbone. My thumb scrolls, about to land on the only other person who could pick me up, when my phone dies.

"Excellent," I mutter, shoving the useless device into my bag before sliding it over my shoulder.

Luckily the crime rate is particularly low in Mayson Ridge, so it's the only reason I'm even considering walking these darkened streets alone when it's nearing midnight. Most of the time on a Friday night downtown would be buzzing, but it's show season, and for towns like mine it means that everyone is gone north to Ft. Worth. Including my parents and my older brothers, which is why Brady was designated my ride since my car is in the shop.

My aching feet carry me past the Mayson Jar's neon sign, and past the entrance of the hardware store, until I'm standing next to the small, faded brick building that's been empty since I've been alive. The large picture window would be a perfect spot to display buckets of wildflowers and other floral arrangements. Especially the ones I pick in the pasture at the east end of the ranch.

Lost in my secret daydream, the sound of an engine pulls my attention away and I turn to see a familiar Chevy truck idle up next to me. The driver side door flies open, revealing a tall, broad-shouldered cowboy, with a scowl planted on his handsome face that's barely visible beneath the brim of a black Stetson hat.

"What the fuck, Ivy?" His deep voice rumbles through my chest like a violent earthquake.

Maddox Sheppard, my inconsiderate boyfriend's older brother stalks toward me, peeling his coat off in the process. "What are you doing out here this late? It's freezing."

I blink, my breath stuttering as I watch the man that I've known just as long as Brady, completely remove his Cinch jacket before draping it over my shoulders.

"Get in the truck," he commands; his tone hard like it usually is when he's around me.

But I'm hungry, cold, and have no desire to dig deep enough to muster up the energy to argue. I allow him to usher me to the passenger side, where he opens the door and helps me climb in. When he hops in the driver seat, slamming his door, I finally manage to speak.

"I can't get a hold of Brady." I wave my phone between us. "Then my phone died."

His jaw clenches as he grips the steering wheel before peeling one hand off to grab the charger that's hazardously coiled in the floor of the truck. "He was supposed to pick you up?" He asks as he hands it my way.

"Yeah. We talked about it this morning." I plug my phone in before dropping it on the bench seat.

His eyes close, his head shaking as he mutters a string of curse words under his breath. The truck shifts into drive, and the cab grows silent.

"You know where he is?" I ask.

I cast a glance at his profile. He and Brady may be brothers, but they only favor in terms of hair color. Maddox has piercing hazel eyes, like their mother, while Brady has light honey brown like their father. You'd have to be diagnosed legally blind not to see that Maddox is as handsome as they come.

"He went to Shreveport with Clay. They left about noon," he finally says, irritation lacing his tone. "Clay has two rides tonight."

A rodeo. He ditched me for a freaking rodeo he's not even riding in.

"I don't know why I even keep doing this," I say aloud.

"There's no excuse, Ivy," he grits out.

I swallow, knowing he's right. Maddox never was one to sugarcoat. He meant the things he said, and even though he always seemed pissed off at anyone and everything, I knew deep down it was because he cared.

More than I can say for his brother.

We ride out to my family's ranch without another word spoken. As subtly as I can, I use the darkness to snuggle into his jacket, letting the hint of spice mingled with the scent of fresh soap comfort me. It smells like home and masculinity. It smells like a man.

When we pull up to the old farmhouse, the lights are off, the stillness showing not a soul is in sight.

"You staying alone?" His eyes are on the house, his brow furrowed.

"Mom, dad, Cooper, and Ryder are gone. But Clyde is in the bunkhouse," I say as I unclip my seatbelt.

"I don't like it," he bites out.

I let out a light laugh. "I'll be fine. No one can get through the gates anyway."

Maddox unfolds himself from the seat of the truck, stepping out, before he's rounding the hood. I have the door halfway open, but he catches it, offering me his hand.

"I'll walk you." He nods.

Maddox wasn't a man of many words, but he didn't need them. His actions seemed to always speak in their place. Which is why we kind of had our own language. I would get in some sort of bind, where Brady was typically at fault, and Maddox would randomly show up and save the day. Just like tonight.

We step onto the wrap around porch, and I use my house key to open the door. I crack the it before I reach up and remove his jacket. I immediately miss the warmth but reluctantly hand it over.

"Thank you." I give a small smile, suddenly feeling embarrassed over the fact my boyfriend forgot me. Again.

"Give me your phone." He holds out a large palm.

I track his eyes as they cautiously watch me place my phone in his hand. His thick fingers quickly type something out, before he hands it back.

"If you ever need me. Call."

Hazel eyes narrow on mine, waiting for a verbal response.

"Ok." I swallow thickly.

He nods again, leaving me standing at the door as he walks to his truck.

I don't even bother turning on any lights. I go straight upstairs, take a shower, then crawl into bed.

I'm sound asleep when a distant rumble wakes me. Rolling over, I check my phone to see it's five in the morning. Curious, I creep across the cold wooden floor, then peer out from in between my white lace curtains. A swirl of something I've never felt sparks deep inside of my chest when I see Maddox slowly backing out of the driveway to leave the ranch.

He stayed all night?

Reaching for my phone, I scroll down to his contact that he put in just a few hours ago, then type out a text.

Ivy: You didn't have to stay.

Maddox: I know.

But he stayed anyway.

Chapter One

Ivy

Present day

The parking lot to Simpson Memorial Hospital is eerie at this time of night. Nothing but a few random birds and a doctor in a white lab coat taking a smoke break. *Ironic.* My swift steps carry me across the pavement, my nerves curled tight in the pit of my stomach. Exactly sixteen hours ago I received at text from my brother, Cooper.

You need to come home.

I stared at the words, debating on whether to ignore what I assumed was just another attempt to get me back to Texas, but the following text had my world shifting on its axis.

There was a fire. Dad is in the hospital.

Dread had almost swallowed me whole, but instead of surrendering to the *what if's*, I shoved aside all of the reasons why I left Mayson Ridge four years ago. I shoved them far enough away to manage to pack a bag, jump in my car, and hit the road without a deep dive into what shitstorm would be waiting for me.

The drive was long, exhausting, and my hands were sore from gripping the steering wheel for hours on end. I had my reasons for leaving, and honestly, I didn't have any plans to return any time soon. So, my sudden reappearance will not only be unexpected, but I'm sure will stir up the gossip mill of our small town.

The sliding glass doors open automatically, creating a breeze that dances through my hair that I didn't even bother brushing. Stepping up to the front counter, my heart thuds wildly, matching the rhythm of a stampede of mustangs like the ones I watched in awe the last time I visited Wyoming.

"Emmett Mayson," I ask.

The grey-haired receptionist doesn't even glance up, her fingers moving furiously over the keyboard in front of her.

"Third floor. Room 316."

Her phone rings, and she answers, still completely ignoring my presence.

I mutter a brief "thank you" before I'm striding to the elevator and pressing the button to the third floor.

The yellow number indicating my arrival causes my eyes to close. *Four years.* I hadn't been in the same room, let alone the same state as my family in almost four years. There were weekly phone calls, but visits were nonexistent. Mostly excuses from me and frustration from them. When the door opens, I step out into the waiting room, my eyes sliding over the handful of people that are hunkered down in uncomfortable chairs waiting for news on their loved ones.

My gaze lands on a mop of sandy brown hair that's tilted back against the wall. His jeans are stained, with what appears to be mud and soot, which also covers his boots and his cowboy hat that's resting on his knee.

My throat tightens as I take measured steps over to my brother.

"Coop," I croak.

His eyes peel open, exhaustion and worry residing in the blue hue that matches our mother's.

"Ivy." He leans up, pushing to his feet. "You came."

I nod, tears stinging my eyes as he wraps his arms around my shoulders, pulling me in for a hug. He smells like smoke, the musk almost causing me to cough before he pulls away. "He's alright. Smoke inhalation, a concussion, and some minor burns. But he's alive."

I swallow past the lump in my throat. "What happened?"

He rakes a hand through his hair. "I'm not sure exactly. The back four pastures caught fire, along with the big house."

The big house

Our childhood home. The one that holds all the memories. The stories. The secrets.

"Is it...." I trail off.

The look in his eyes tell me what I don't want to hear.

"It's gone, Ives," he says hoarsely.

"Where's mom?" I ask, my hands clinging to the strap on my purse.

"She's in the room with dad. She wasn't home. Thank God." He motions. "You want to see him?"

Do I? No. Not really. Not yet. I haven't looked into his eyes in years. It was too hard. But this was serious. He was hurt. *And still my father.*

"Yeah. I'd like to see him," I finally answer, my voice quiet.

He nods, and wraps an arm around my shoulder, guiding me toward the hall. Just as we round the corner, a tall body meets us head on. I halt my steps, letting the angry eyes of my oldest brother slice right through my heart.

"What are you doing here?" He asks, his words harsh causing me to almost wince.

"I asked her to be here," Cooper interjects.

"Ryder..." I begin but he cuts me off.

"Is this what it takes for you to come home? A fucking tragedy?" He grits out.

My cheeks flame, my pulse racing. "That's not fair."

"Fair?" He scoffs. "What's not fair is you abandoning your family."

"I never abandoned anyone," I snap.

But didn't you, Ivy?

"Bullshit," he barks.

His thunderous voice bounces off of the empty walls of the hallway, earning us a warning glare from the charge nurse.

"This isn't the place, Ryder." Cooper maneuvers me ahead of him. "Cool off. It's been a long day and this ain't helping."

With that we brush past him, walking silently to the end of the hallway.

"It's here." Cooper presses the silver lever, opening the door to a small dim room.

Entering with lead feet, I walk slowly until I'm standing next to the aging man lying in the hospital bed. His eyes are closed while an oxygen mask is strapped over his face. It's paired with a white bandage around his head. The sounds of the monitors give off a steady beat as Wheel of Fortune plays softly in the background from the tv that's mounted on the wall. It hurts. Seeing him like this.

A toilet flushes and the door to the bathroom opens before the best person I've ever known joins me.

My mother.

When her eyes land on me, she sucks in a sharp breath, and her voice cracks.

"Ivy."

"Hey mama." My words are just as shredded as hers, and it's even more evident in this moment that those four years of absence had done nothing to ease the guilt I took along with me. The guilt I was hoping I could bury somewhere else.

Chapter Two

Ivy

"Let's talk out in the hall so we don't wake him," my mom whispers in my ear.

"I'll stay with him." Cooper places a kiss on my mom's head before taking a seat in the blue chair next to dad's bed.

When we close the door behind us, my mother lets out a compressed sob.

"I thought we were going to lose him," she admits.

Her painful cry splits my already marred heart farther in two. "He's ok mom."

She lets out a breath, her hands shaking as she reaches for mine. "Situation aside. I'm so glad you're here, sweetheart." Her hands squeeze. "I missed you."

Damn this place. I've been here all of five minutes and I'm on the verge of torrential tears. "I missed you too, mom."

I have missed her. Missed my brother's, my best friends, my *home.* But sometimes it's not enough to erase the pain.

"What did the doctor say?" I ask.

Her blonde hair is swept back, her eyes shining as she sniffs. "We're waiting for him to come back. They did another CT scan. We are hoping for no swelling or bleeding on the brain."

My father was a pillar of this community. Our family was known for generations of hard-working ranchers. I don't think the man had been to a doctor's office in his entire life. Honestly, when he wakes up, I feel sorry for the nurses and hospital staff. The only person to ever check him out for any ranch related injuries was Dr. Palmer, our vet.

"He's strong, mom," I remind her.

"I know." She glances up, blinking her eyes. "Lord knows he's as stubborn as an ox."

I let a slight chuckle slip past my lips at the fact that she still held her sense of humor.

"How was the drive? You must be tired."

Of course she's worried about me. Not the fact our lively hood could be completely destroyed.

"Don't worry about me. How are you doing? What do you need?" I ask, my gaze meeting hers.

"I'm ok." She flicks her hand over her shirt. "I don't need much. My kids all in one place and your father healthy is all I need."

Her arms reach out for me again, tugging me close as she sways us side to side. "Thank you."

I nod, unable to form words.

"Why don't you go check on your brother." She tilts her head in the direction of the waiting room.

"I don't think Ryder wants to talk to me." I fiddle with the hem of my shirt. "He's angry."

She rolls her eyes. "He'll get over it. You know how he is. Anger is his choice of emotion when he doesn't know how to sort out his feelings."

Typical man.

"I'll let you know when the doctor gives us an update," she offers.

"Ok."

With one more squeeze, she opens the door, speaking in a low voice to Cooper. Breathing out the heavy emotions twisting inside of me, I make my way back to the waiting room. Ryder sits in the corner, his broad frame almost too big for the chair. Like Cooper, it's clear they were in the middle of the turmoil. He's covered in residue as well, his worn hat resting low on his head, covering his eyes.

Taking a seat next to him, I peek out of the corner of my eye, but he doesn't move, nor does he speak right away. I'm not sure if he's asleep, or just ignoring me, but my question is answered when he rumbles from beneath his hat.

"That seat is taken."

Home sweet home.

Chapter Three

Ivy

I must have dosed. The next thing I knew I was prying my eyes open to see Cooper crouched down in front of me.

"Hey. They just told us the doctor won't be by until tomorrow morning. It's already almost midnight. Why don't you go back to the ranch and rest. You can come back tomorrow."

I frown, my fingers reaching up to rub the sleep from my eyes.

"But mom," I start.

"Mom insisted." He stands. "And we both know she doesn't like it when we don't listen. I'll stay out here."

He has a point.

"I'll walk you out," he adds.

Gathering my purse, I follow him out of the waiting room. It's empty, so I'm assuming Ryder has already left. We make it down the elevator and into the parking lot.

"You can just stay in Houston's old room at the cabin. It's empty." He grips me in a hug. "Watch for deer."

I almost roll my eyes, but the fact Cooper is being his usual, protective self makes the anxiety built up in my muscles ease a little.

"I will. Call me the second you hear anything."

After climbing back into my car, and the thirty minute drive to the ranch, I can barely keep my eyes open. I manage to make it to the cabin that Cooper has lived in since he turned eighteen. Letting myself inside, I sluggishly slide my feet to the bedroom, dropping my bag on the floor before I'm crawling under the covers and letting the exhaustion finally take over.

A sharp ray of light hits my face, causing me to groan out my frustration. I hadn't slept that hard in weeks, and getting out of bed was the last thing I wanted to do. But I had things to do today. People to face. Fears to conquer. Sliding out from underneath the covers, I pad into the kitchen in search of a coffee pot. One is placed on the counter, so I quickly start what will be my life saver today then resort to the bathroom for a hot shower. After scalding my skin, and possibly ruining the hair mask I did last week by using whatever dollar store shampoo and soap combination Cooper had on the shelf, I shut off the water and step out onto the bath mat. Shivering, I toss open the cabinet above the toilet, my hand searching for a clean towel. My fingers meet solid wood, not the plush material I assumed would be there. Gritting my teeth, I stomp to the door, peeking out towards the laundry room. It's just a few steps away, and knowing my brother, the towels are still in the dryer, most likely having been tumbled at least three times by now. Laundry was never his strong suit. Honestly, I wouldn't be surprised if my mother still comes over and does it for him.

Tiptoeing across the old wood floors, the air conditioning kicks on, which causes my nipples to peak immediately. I curse under my breath, rounding the corner with a skid, before I collide into a solid wall of muscle. A surprised scream erupts from my throat as I stumble back, but a warm callused hand catches my upper arm. My eyes finally raise, traveling up the broad chest, before they lock with a pair of blazing hazel eyes. Eyes I've seen give me this same look hundreds of times. Eyes that I wish belonged to anyone else. Anyone else besides Maddox Sheppard. Those angry eyes dip down, raking over me, reminding me that I'm not only naked, but soaking wet. I rip away, one arm covering my boobs, while the other hand shoots down to cover everything south.

"What the hell are you doing here?" I hiss, backing away.

"Me?" He lifts a brow. "You're the one in my house."

"You're house?" I frown in confusion. "This is Cooper's cabin."

He never moves from the hallway, his gaze still hard and unwavering.

"I'm assuming Copper didn't tell you that he moved into the apartment above the barn two years ago. I live here now."

I want to die. Crawl inside a hole with some rabid coyote family and let them rip me to pieces so I don't have to live through this mortification.

"I..." I shake my head, my hands still covering the goods as I take another step backwards.

"Watch the..." Maddox begins, but it's too late.

My ankle catches on the corner of a saddle that's inconveniently tossed in the floor, and I tumble down, landing flat on my naked ass.

My hands instinctively leave my body to break my fall, exposing every intimate part of me to the man I would have gladly given myself to on a silver platter years ago, but that was no longer the case.

"Damn it, Ivy," he grits out before he's storming in my direction.

Before I can stand, I'm yanked up and tossed over his shoulder. He rounds the corner to the bedroom, where I'm thrown down onto the bed like a useless sack of Idaho potatoes. The door slams, and I remain motionless. Breathless. Embarrassed.

The door cracks open again, and a towel comes flying in my direction. Before I can respond with a weak *thank you*, he slams it again, causing the house to practically shake from its force.

You can always go home they said.

Well, *they,* were full of shit.

Chapter Four

Ivy

Twenty minutes later I'm dressed and glaring at Cooper from the front porch of the cabin.

"Really Cooper? You failed to mention you don't even live here anymore."

He shrugs. "Sorry, I forgot. What happened?"

"I'd rather not relive it," I hiss as I move down the stairs, falling in line with him.

I forgot how alive this place looks in the early mornings. The sounds of the birds. The colors of the sky when the sun rises just above the ridges. The continuous rustling of the animals at the barn. Which thank the Lord, is still standing. It's weird how you take it for granted. The simple things. Angry car horns during rush hour have been the only serenade I've been privy to for the last few years. Not the songs of nature.

With smooth steps I follow Cooper out past the old horse barn. This ranch is over ten thousand acres, and I hadn't seen anything remotely this breath taking in my time in Georgia. I don't think I ever will.

But as we walk, I begin to see the remnants of what was previously prime pastureland, and the charred wood of what use to be a happy home.

"Well. Go ahead." I gesture my hand, waiting for the lecture deep down I know I deserve. "Tell me how pissed you are."

Cooper pulls out a toothpick and shoves it in his mouth. "Don't get me wrong, I'm mad as fuck that you've not even bothered to show your face in four years, but I'm glad to see you."

Cooper and I always had a special relationship. He had that energy about him. He was a natural peace maker. He wasn't your stereotypical middle child. He was the life of the party, but he also had a soft side only a few got to see.

"I know y'all are angry. I didn't visit," I admit.

"Visit?" He scoffs. "You fell off the face of the earth, Ivy."

I close my eyes.

"I know you had dreams to chase. Hell, I encouraged it. I just always thought you'd come back." His eyes soften as he approaches the fence line, completely ignoring the house.

This pasture, which is no longer a beautiful green, but a black pit, borders my favorite wildflower field and I feel that heavy weight in my chest return. I know what's next to that field. And another wave of emotion hits because the fire didn't touch it.

"Well. I'm here," I say simply as we stare out among the fields that still harbor a visible layer of smoke.

"How long did it take them?" I ask.

"Right before we left to come home, chief called and said they had it contained and mostly out. They had been working on it for over twenty-four hours."

"How many acres?" I keep my eyes trained on the open range.

"About three thousand. Give or take." He lifts a shoulder. "Some cattle got swept up in it. The hay is gone."

Damn. That's a big hit.

"It's bad, isn't it?" I whisper.

He lets out a breath. "Yeah. It's bad."

He rests a forearm along the pipe railing. "You really like the city?" His question throws me, but I'm assuming a subject change is what he needs. This land is Cooper's baby, and it's obvious he's struggling.

I let out a breath, letting my eyes drift over the field of flowers.

"It has its perks," I answer.

I watch him search my face. "Come on, Ivy it's me."

I snort a laugh. "It's not this *hot* for one."

We both stare out into the untouched pasture, watching the yellows and pinks sway with the light breeze. A decent breeze is a rare occasion in this part of Texas.

He doesn't ask me anymore questions or hammer me about why I never visited. We just simply stand there, trying to grasp onto whatever this means for our family.

"You call Kota?" He asks.

"I sent her a text. I wasn't sure if she was here or not."

He nods. "Yeah. Her trailer is parked out by the arena."

I lean my head down on his shoulder. "Thanks Coop." I feel his head rest against mine. "And I'm sorry I left you," I admit.

"I know. I forgave you a long time ago." He brings up his palm to squeeze my shoulder. "But right now, we need you."

I nod, knowing that this isn't something I can just run away from. Not this time. His phone pings, and I wrap my arms around my middle.

"Ryder needs me. We have to shift the herd around. Give me a couple of hours and I can take you to town to see dad."

"That's fine." I tilt my head. "I thought I'd pay Sugarfoot a visit."

Cooper leans over, dropping a kiss on the top of my head. "She'd like that."

Sliding on his sunglasses, he veers off to the left of the barn toward the main office, while I turn in the opposite direction, heading to the horses. It was my favorite place on the property. Well, it used to be before tainted memories filled the space. But I could ignore those. I *had been for years*, and I could really use some equine soothing in this moment.

Stepping inside the freshly remodeled barn, I pass two empty stalls, ignoring the room to my right until I come to the one that I've visited more times than I can count.

"Hey sweet girl," I coo as I peer over at Sugarfoot.

Her long dark mane looks smooth and shiny, like it's been brushed daily. She appears happy and healthy and that's all I could ask for. Tears prick my eyes over the fact I haven't been the one to do it. I abandoned her too.

I reach my hand out to press my palm against her neck, slowly running it up and down as her big brown eyes catch on mine.

"It's been a while," I whisper. "I'm sorry."

An unexpected wave of fresh goose bumps dance over my skin, and I already know without having to look who just walked into this barn.

Chapter Five

Maddox

I'm tired.

Pissed.

And now fully erect.

Ivy's bare perfect ass was inches from my face and now I'm suffering the consequences.

I have my phone in hand, ready to call Coop when his name flashes across the screen.

"Anything you need to tell me?" I bark into the phone.

"Awe shit. You ran into Ivy?" He asks.

Ran into?

"Something like that," I mutter.

"Sorry I forgot to text you to let you know she was going to stay in the extra bedroom. I don't have any room in the loft and Ryder...well, he's not exactly giving her a warm welcome."

I sigh, pinching the bridge of my nose. I've been up all night, staying out with the crew while the fire department did their job. They wanted someone from the ranch present, and seeing as he and Ryder needed to be with Emmett, it was a no brainer.

"It's fine." I drop my hand.

Is it though?

"It's just for a few days as of now." He goes on. "I know she's been gone a while, but it's time she puts whatever bullshit aside with this place long enough to get through this mess."

I nod, even though I know that he can't see me as I walk aimlessly around the grounds with no particular destination in mind. I need to walk off this boner for starters.

"How's Emmett?" I ask.

"No word yet. I just got back. I need to shit, shower, then get out there with Ryder to move pastures."

"Thanks for the warning." Pocketing my phone, I take a few minutes to survey the demolished structure of the farmhouse before I turn around and head to the horse barn.

I step inside, and all the progress that I had made on the walk over here flies out the window.

Ivy Mayson stands before me, transporting me back to the years when I would try to pretend that I wasn't gawking at her while I shoveled horse shit from these very stalls.

Her hand is smoothing over Sugarfoot's mane as she leans over the stall gate.

"It's been a while," she whispers. "I'm sorry."

The pain in her voice makes me uncomfortable, so I clear my throat.

Her head whips in my direction and she straightens abruptly. She's fully clothed now, so I can appreciate the woman in front of me without feeling like complete shit. I was shocked to see her. Not only shocked to see her naked body, but to be in her presence in general. Her pink lip's part when she spins around, the ones that have always intrigued me. Her top lip is slightly fuller than the bottom, never seizing to tempt me to snag it beneath my teeth. But because I was born with fucking morals, and my younger brother Brady dated her through the better part of their teenage years, I never crossed the line. I had too much respect for Ivy and even though Brady was a little shit with his own issues, and frankly didn't deserve her, he was still my brother. Regardless of his tendency to manipulate those around him, I loved him. I would never do anything to intentionally hurt him.

Back then Ivy was young. Too young, and I was just a summer ranch hand, while she had dreams. Goals larger than life. I remember that beautiful smile, with those alluring green eyes that reminded me of the wildflower fields she spent the majority of her time in. She used to be the girl in pigtails with a small gap between her top teeth, then one summer, when she turned sixteen, she.... wasn't, and as a grown ass man, I had no business noticing. No business wondering what it would be like to kiss the lips of my brother's girl. It was fucked up, but I couldn't help it. She was good all the way down to her soul and it took everything I had not to pummel my brother for taking it for granted. But on the outside, you wouldn't know. I kept my mask in place. Especially when it concerned Ivy Mayson.

But here she stood in the flesh. No longer his girl. All grown up and *back.* In Texas. I almost forgot how angry I was at her for leaving her entire family in the dust. *Including me.* Not even a fucking goodbye.

"Maddox," she says cooly.

My eyes casually scan across her frame. She's still just as beautiful as the last time I saw her. The day she came rolling into the ranch and refused to even speak to me, which had me consecutively drunk off my ass for the following three days. Her smile was still for someone else, and it made me sick.

I try not to but fail miserably when my gaze involuntarily casts down to her wrist and I'd be lying if I said something didn't hit me square in the chest when I saw this simple wildflower tattoo. *What did it mean?*

Why the fuck do you care, Sheppard? You practically ripped her heart out and sent her away.

"I see you decided to dress accordingly," I point out.

Her brows furrow, ignoring my attempt at being an ass. "Why are you here?"

I tilt my head, a little amused at the fact she has no idea. "I work here."

"You still work the summers here?" She questions.

I lift a brow. "I manage the bulls and the breeding contracts."

Her hands fall to her sides, and she forces a fake smile. "That's great."

I reach down and hook my thumbs in my pockets. Her demeanor is weird, and I don't like it. "Been about two and a half years now."

She nods.

"Ryder called you?" I ask.

She shakes her head. "Coop."

"Doesn't surprise me."

"Why because he's the only one that seems to give a shit about me?" There's an edge to her voice, one that has me wondering what caused it. Ivy was always confident, but never snappy.

"Why you say that?" I press.

"Ryder isn't happy. He's been very clear how he feels about my absence. I guess you two share the same opinion of me. Considering you were always so far up his ass if you spit out your Copenhagen it was coming out of his mouth."

An uncontainable scoff barks from my chest. This is the Ivy I remember. "I have my opinions, and they are mine alone."

"Yeah, well sorry about earlier." Her cheeks flush. "You don't have to worry about it happening again. I won't be staying there."

Which is probably for the best. And the fact we are standing in the exact place that everything between us fell apart is not lost on me. On one hand so much has changed, and on the other, *nothing* has changed.

She's still untouchable.

She's still my brother's ex.

And unfortunately, I still had to be the asshole who broke her heart.

Chapter Six

Ivy

Maddox *motherfucking* Sheppard.

He *works* here. Full time.

I stomp across the freshly cut grass, cursing under my breath the entire way to the arena.

I didn't get to take him in this morning, I was too busy trying my hardest not to flash my naked ass to God and everyone. Then I was too busy putting on a front of indifference. His dark hair still slightly curled at the ends, like it was fresh from the shower, and it still poked out from beneath his straw cowboy hat. His jeans still molded to those strong thighs that were evidence of the many miles he's ridden on this ranch. His stubbled jaw was still as sharp as his last words to me, and those damn hazel eyes still made my pulse thud uncontrollably beneath the skin on my neck. He was the same, yet different. He was older. Rougher, and still the man I would forever feel guilty for loving.

The reasons I stayed states away from this place for so long seem to be slamming right into my face this morning. No easing into the memories left behind. Nope. Those are making a cold as ice welcome, and I can already feel the frostbite.

I hate the way my heart fluttered at the sound of his voice. That smooth rumble that always made my stomach drop since I understood what it meant when my heart would begin to race when he merely entered a room. I believe the first time I felt it I was seventeen, and I soon realized that my four-year relationship with Brady was filled with nothing but easy friendship, and excuses. Excuses of why he partied so much. Excuses of why he was talking to that girl from San Antonio or the one from the rodeo the previous weekend that he attended without me. I cared for Brady, and we made social sense. Your typical cheerleader dates the football captain. Eventually, I realized how unfair it was to Brady that my feelings for him were practically nonexistent, and the breakup wasn't as smooth as I had hoped. Brady being himself, threw a couple of tantrums to get my attention. *To guilt me* into taking him back. But I was done. Done long before I said the words out loud. But as time went on, my innocent crush on his older brother soon bloomed into full blown feelings, in which he was very clear he didn't have for me after the night I childishly humiliated myself. I took his protective nature as a possibility that he saw me as more than just a young girl. I thought when he held me in his arms and told me he would rip apart anyone who ever hurt me, that he meant it. When he told me I could call him anytime, no matter what, and he would answer, that I held more of a place in his life than just his little brother's naive ex-girlfriend. But boy was I dead wrong, and my heart still has the deep set crack to prove it.

Finally, the arena comes into view, and I spot the faded red Bloomer trailer parked on the left side of the dingy white fence. I swing my leg over the pipe railing, then follow the path around to the trailer door. A small smile forms on my lips when I read the sign that's hung with a piece of vet tape.

If it's before 8am. Fuck off.

(Yes, that means you, Cooper)

Dakota Sterling was the freest of souls. This nomadic gypsy I secretly envied. I loved her ability to have zero reservations about what anyone else thought about her. I admired it, and the fact it was indeed before eight, had me grinning, despite the despair around us. When I pound a fist against the trailer door, I hear a groan, followed by some obscene foul language, then the heavy steps of a pissed off Dakota. The door is barely ajar when she starts spitting her venom.

"I swear to God, Cooper. I already told you; I don't want your shit coffee."

The door fully slings open, revealing a barefoot figure, with long black unruly hair. A Whitney Houston crop top stops just above her pierced navel, and a pair of pink spandex shorts cover her lower half.

"Does he still actually think it tastes good?" I ask as I cross my arms.

Her eyes widen, and the scowl slides into a shocked but genuine smile.

"You dirty little skank." She reaches out, wrapping a long arm around my neck, crashing our top halves together. The position is awkward as I hover over the makeshift *stair* to the trailer, which is a strategically placed Yeti cooler.

"I'm so pissed at you." She releases me. Kisses my forehead, then jerks me inside, slamming the door behind me. "Get in here before Cooper sees I'm up. He'll make me help saddle the horses."

I snicker, knowing secretly that Cooper will saddle the horses for her regardless. Dakota may be clueless to my brother's clear affection for her, but I'm not. The only reason we became close friends is because he was friends with her first. I just kind of stole her away. Truth be told she prefers him over me, though her stubbornness would never allow her to admit it.

"Does Laiken know you're home?" She opens a plastic tub, pulling out a pair of washed-out jeans.

"Not yet." I take a seat on a pile of outdated rodeo magazines on the couch.

Laiken Sheppard was another piece to our trio that formed when I started dating Brady. Laiken is his sister. Two years older, and we became fast friends that lasted even through the cheating scandals and ultimately the breakup.

"Just move that stuff. I need to toss it anyway," she murmurs as she spins around to change her top. She works the t-shirt over her head before she flips her hair out of the neck and faces me.

"Where the hell have you been, Ivy?" She gathers her hair up to put it in a bun on top of her head. "And what the hell happened with the fire? I was dead asleep when Clyde and Farley came beating the door down."

I sigh. That's a lot to unload. "How about we go to breakfast with Laiken? We can talk then. I would like to bring mom some food and clothes back to the hospital."

She purses her lips but finally nods. "Fine. But you're buying. Serves you right for ghosting us."

There's a lightness in her tone, but the truth of it presses on my chest. We Face Timed and talked as often as we could, but it wasn't the same, and being back here for the short time I have tells me that *nothing* may ever be the same.

Chapter Seven

Ivy

Dakota peels out from the only red light in Mayson Ridge just in time to completely cut off Laiken's SUV, causing her to skid to a stop. Her window immediately rolls down, her mouth ready to give Dakota the what for when she spots me.

"Ivy!" She gasps.

I wiggle my fingers. "Hey Laik."

Dakota taps the side of her truck. "Breakfast at the Mayson Jar. Meet us there."

"But I have yoga before work." Laiken's face morphs into clear distress.

Laiken has always been the rule follower. The quiet one. The small notion of skipping a meaningless yoga class might cause her to go into cardiac arrest. She almost did when she found out she was pregnant with her adorable son Trace. She spiraled for days until she finally heard his heartbeat. The rest was history.

"Your ass is perfect, Red." Dakota winks. "Chop chop."

Laiken's response is muffled by the sound of squealing tires and a blaring horn from the other side of the intersection.

When the window is rolled up, I can't help but grin. *I missed this.*

"What?" Dakota reaches for the dial, cranking up the radio to an ungodly volume.

"Nothing." I wave her off, tilting my head back to rest on the seat and decide I can do nothing but let George Strait lead us to breakfast.

As expected, when the three of us enter the Mayson Jar, all heads turn. A few jaws drop, and a couple of eyes give me a bewildered look of pity.

"Ivy Mayson." Fern taps her red press on nails against the hostess stand. "It's been a while. Sorry to hear about the fire."

I nod, giving her a similar version a of a smile. "Thanks Fern."

She picks up a few menus. "I heard the fire department spent all night out there. Took the team from two towns over to help get it under control."

"Yeah. I don't know many details yet. I got in late last night."

We take a seat at a corner table, the one that sits beneath a large stuffed buffalo.

"How's that little cowboy of yours?" Fern asks Laiken.

"Growing like a weed. I can't believe he just turned six." She grins as she takes a menu into her hands.

Fern's gaze then lands on Dakota, her eyes narrowing. "Ms. Sterling."

She leaves the table while Dakota tosses a smile and the bird to her back.

"Have I told y'all lately how much I hate my last name?" She mutters.

Her tone is full of sarcasm, but it doesn't hide the deep set hurt in her eyes. Dakota didn't exactly grow up with an ideal family. Her being born into a name that holds a bad reputation in this town hasn't done her any favors. Regardless of her severing ties with her father who's currently serving a ten-year sentence in the Cove County Prison, people just assume the apple doesn't fall far from the tree.

"Your dad doing ok?" Laiken leads the conversation away from Dakota's unconventional family. Which judging by the look on her face, she's thankful for.

"He's alive. We are waiting on the results from a second CT scan. Me and Cooper left about midnight. I planned to grab mom some essentials before I go back to get the update."

"It was chaos," Dakota says. "When Clyde was freaking out, I knew it was bad. That man is usually as slow as molasses."

"He's pushing seventy," Laiken nudges her. "Give the man a break."

Dakota rolls her eyes. "The horses were terrified. Thank God, it didn't make it to that side of the property, but they knew something was off." She shakes her head. "I tried to get the hose on the house when I realized the fire had hit the porch, but your brother flipped shit."

"He was right to." I give her a pointed look.

"I was just trying to help. Cooper literally hauled me to the apartment and made me stay inside. He was all; she lowers her voice to mock him. "*Sit your ass in this chair and don't you fucking move, Kota.*"

Laiken and I share a look, the same one we've shared for years.

"I watched out the window mostly. Maddox ran into the house. Got your dad out."

My heart drops. "He ran inside?"

She nods. "Yeah. Carried him out over his shoulder. It was wild."

He saved my father?

Emotion hits me again; the reality he could have been hurt triggers feelings that I had hoped to compress.

"I'm just glad everyone is ok." Laiken reaches across the table to grip my hand and for a second I almost flinch, remembering the fact that I was naked in front of her brother less than two hours ago. *The one I didn't date.* "And I'm glad you're home. We missed you, Ives."

"I missed you too." I smile.

The door to the kitchen swings open, showcasing my aunt Penelope with hands planted on her curvy hips.

"Ivy Ruth Mayson." Her tone is scolding, but a smile is fixated on her face. "You come into my restaurant and not even hug my neck?"

Slipping from my seat, I meet her halfway, tossing my arms around my mother's younger sister.

"It's good to see you baby girl." She squeezes me tight. "How's your mama?"

I pull back. "She's ok. Tired. Worried."

Her hands rub up and down my arms. "I'll get Kenny to make you girls the special, and I'll make to go plates for your mom and Emmett. We all know that hospital food is hog wash."

I chuckle. "That sounds great."

She glances over my shoulder and winks, her fake lashes fluttering as she does. "Fire chief just walked in." She wags her brows. "He just hit the six month post-divorce mark. Time to put the new girls to work."

Most would think she means *waitresses.* But this is Penelope, so she discreetly shimmies her very new and very large breast implants at me. A laugh bubbles from my throat.

I guess some things never change.

Chapter Eight

Maddox

I brace my hands on the fence as Ryder approaches me on horseback.

"How many?" I ask.

He maneuvers his old bay horse parallel to the railing, then removes the bandana from over his mouth.

"We've lost thirty head so far."

"Fuck," I hiss. "Yeah. We got Clyde, Farley, and Aiden coming from the back side. Hoss and Waylon are on the east end trying to get a head count and see the damage."

I remove my sunglasses, squinting as Cooper comes riding in from the right. "The pasture bordering the Bernard's is clear."

Ryder leans his forearm down on his saddle horn. "We still have over a thousand acres to check."

"Shit." Cooper fishes his phone out of his pocket. "I thought we'd cover more ground quicker. Ivy went to breakfast with Kota. I told her I'd take her to the hospital."

"Can't she just uber? Isn't that what they do in the city?" Ryder mutters under his breath.

"You're a dick, you know that?" Cooper nudges his horse closer to Ryder. "She's your sister. Get your panties out of your ass and forgive her. She's not Hadley."

Ryder's jaw clenches and with one swift kick of his boot he takes off.

"Grumpy motherfucker," Cooper scoffs.

"Really Coop?" I step back from the fence. "You had to go there?"

"Someone needs to call him on his shit."

I shake my head, turning to travel back to the office. Luckily all the bucking bulls are kept in a separate area of the property along with the breeding barn which has been my domain for the last two years.

On the way to my office, a Mayson Ridge fire department truck pulls up. My brother Brady, along with Dobs, another Mayson Ridge fireman step out.

Brady adjusts his cap before he nods at me. "How are things this morning?"

I shove my hands in my pockets with a shrug. "About the same as last night. Burned all to hell."

Brady spent about three years chasing tail and staying drunk before he decided to get it together. It was slowly killing our mother, and after some serious talks and even a night in jail, he finally got his head out of his ass and applied for the fire academy. It's the best thing he ever did for himself, and the last few months have been smoother. Less tension and more conversation like it used to be before the accident that catastrophically hit our family.

"Chief wanted us to do a recheck. He'll be sending someone out later to do the inspection and determine the cause."

We fall in step with each other as I lead them over to the side by side.

"You can take this. Key is in the cup holder."

"Thanks man." He slaps my shoulder. "Beers later this week?"

I know my face shows surprise because his expression turns solemn.

"Sure," I agree. "I'll swing by after I stop by mom's. She needs her filters changed."

They take off toward the scene of the crime while I head to my office. I can already feel the tightness in my chest. That ache that's been persistent for the last ten fucking years.

I love my brother, but he blames me. And I guess my punishment comes in the form of loving her. It's a vicious circle.

Loving the one woman I can't have. *Because he had her first.*

Chapter Nine

Ivy

I'm sitting next to the hospital bed, staring at the steady rise and fall of my father's chest. Dakota was able to take me by the town market to grab a few things for mom. She hadn't showered in two days, so I volunteered to sit with him while she got cleaned up. There were so many words scrambling around in my brain. So many unsaid things. So many resentments.

With a heavy sigh, I reach for his hand, holding the callused palm against mine.

"I'm sorry I left daddy." I brush my fingers over his knuckles. "But you broke my heart."

The tears threaten to come, but I don't let them. I cried enough four years ago. I feel a light squeeze against my hand, and my eyes flicker up to his face. His eyes are still closed. His face void, but then I see it. The tiny tear that trickles down his tan skin, sliding over his temple.

The door to the bathroom opens, and my mom glides into the room with a smile. I retrieve my hand, pushing to my feet.

"Feel better?" I ask.

"So much better." She places her bag down next to the end of the bed.

"The doctor came in an hour ago. CT scan was clear. No bleeding or swelling, so that's a good sign. He will still be kept until his oxygen levels are stable and also for the burns."

"Ok." I tuck my hair behind my ear. "Anything I can do?"

"Update your brothers." Her hands move to tie her hair in a low bun. "And I would really like if you could do a walk through at the house. I know most of everything is gone, but..." she clears her throat. "There may have been something that didn't get destroyed. I would like to get those things."

"Of course." I lean in to hug her, smelling the fresh coconut from her body wash.

"We'll get through this," she whispers.

"I know."

She releases me and continues. "The fire chief will be doing inspections, and we should know more soon."

She takes a seat in the chair I had just vacated, and after a few seconds, I give one last look at my father before I leave the room.

I stand in what used to be the living room. The room that held the majority of my childhood memories. The days when we laughed. Watched movies. Made bets for who would win the round at the NFR that night. Now all that remains are ashes. I step across a broken beam, and tiptoe along the disintegrated original hardwood floors. So far, I've seen nothing salvageable. Nothing that could be returned to it's original state or even be remotely recognizable.

"Anything?" Cooper calls from across the rubble.

"No." I kick at a half burnt dining chair and brace my hands on my hips. "It's all ruined."

"Great," he mutters. "I can't believe this actually happened."

The only thing still standing is the brick fireplace in the middle of the house. The red bricks are coated in a thick black layer, most of them still securely in place. But what's a fireplace without a house to warm?

"They have insurance, right?" I ask, my mind going to the business side of this tragedy.

I majored in it. Might as well put that degree to good use.

"Yeah. We have farm insurance. I'm not sure the coverage. Dad has had it for years. He's the only one who knows all the details."

I nod, my mind already trying to articulate expenses and payouts. Without it, the ranch would practically be finished. Especially with the pastures that burned. The hay was wiped out. A big part of our income from what I remember, and it ignites a slew of financial questions in the back of my mind.

Maneuvering around the fireplace, I ease forward, skirting around more scattered pieces of charred wood. I dread telling my mom that we couldn't find anything. She's already suffered enough.

I'm two steps down the partially standing stairs of the front porch, when I hear the slam of a car door. My eyes glance up and my heart slams to a screeching halt when a smile stretches across Brady Sheppard's face.

My feet falter, my brows furrowing as he takes three strides to me.

"I heard my girl was back in town."

Before I can throw my arms out to stop him, he sweeps me up in a tight hug, spinning a full circle before planting me back on the dirt. On instinct, my arms reach up to steady myself around his shoulders. He doesn't let go immediately, and just as I'm about to untangle from the unwanted affection, my eyes lock on the man over his shoulder.

Maddox meets my eyes before he pauses, then he turns, and gives me his back as he heads to the running ATV.

Seems like that's the only view he's ever going to give me. His back while he walks away.

Chapter Ten

Maddox

I climb in the ATV.

"Shep," Cooper hollers.

"Be back," I call out before I'm spinning out, heading to my cabin that's just beyond the breeding barns.

I already need a beer, and seeing Ivy in my brother's arms just about sent me over the edge.

Parking up next to the porch, I step off and march inside, almost ripping the fridge door off the hinges as I grip a longneck in my hand.

I twist the top, letting the cold liquid cool the fire in my veins. The fire that burns when I think of her. When I think of how my feelings could hurt my brother. When I think of the accident. My eyes close as I bring the bottle up again. I just need to get through the next few days. I know Ivy still has a life in Georgia. Hell, for all I know she has someone waiting for her. A man who that can love her with everything he has. A man that doesn't have to put her second.

Another pull from my cold beer, then my phone is ringing. Fishing it from my pocket, I glance at the screen and swipe.

"Uncle Mads!"

My nephew's face fills the screen. "Nan said there was a big fire."

"There was buddy." I scratch the scruff on my chin. "But everything is good now."

"Tater Tot is ok?" He asks.

I watch the worry etched across his little face.

"Tater Tot is fine."

I can see the relief melt into his expression. "Wheeeeew." He blows air between his teeth. "I almost wasn't a cowboy anymore."

I chuckle. "What do you mean?"

"You know a cowboy is nothing with no horse, Uncle Mad," he points out.

I swear he's hoarding a sixty-year-old man in his six-year-old body.

"Wise words my man."

"Can I come to the Ranch?" He asks, his eyes hopeful.

"Maybe in a couple of days. We got to get everything cleaned up then you can come spend the day with me."

"What about Havoc?" He asks. "That bastard still kicking?"

I snort a laugh.

"Trace Sheppard," my mother scolds. "You watch your language."

"But he says it!" He pouts. "Ryder too."

"Well, I can smack their back ends just as good as I can yours for that foul mouth."

My mother's face suddenly appears behind Trace, her eyebrows raised.

A reluctant "yes ma'am" comes from me and Trace before she goes back to her previous task.

"Havoc is good," I tell him.

Havoc is our prime bucking bull and Trace's favorite.

"I'm going to ride him one day." His brow grows serious.

"I don't doubt it." I laugh. "I'll call your mom later this week. You be good."

"Ok. Stay punchy."

The call goes black, and I shake my head. *Man, I love that kid.* Laiken has worked her ass off. Being a single mother isn't easy, and I've tried to be as involved and present as I can be for her and Trace.

Placing my phone on the counter, I bring my beer to my lips, savoring the way it temporarily eases the ache. Glancing out the window over the sink, I spot a familiar truck pulling through the gates, and all my hackles rise.

Chapter Eleven

Ivy

I weave my hand through the grass, letting my fingertips dance over the colored flowers for the first time in years. I needed some peace. A reminder of the good things that still exist in this place. Which is why after Brady asked to have lunch with me sometime this week, and I politely tiptoed around an answer, I made my escape out here. My safe haven. I don't want to give him the wrong idea, but I also wouldn't mind catching up with an old friend. But that's all I have to offer him. Friendship.

I pull a gorgeous lavender flower from the ground, twirling the stem in between my thumb and finger. This one will work. Over the years, I'd begun using these to say the things I couldn't. Or didn't have the chance to. I can't count the times Maddox stepped in to cover Brady's ass. He never hung around long enough for a thank you, so I started leaving these as my way of saying *thanks*. Whether it be behind his windshield wipers, on his porch, or the seat of his truck. We may not have always talked, but I was thankful for him anyway. Even though he probably trashed them the second he found them, at least I did my part. I turn to head back to the house, planning to drop these flowers somewhere to say thank you for my dad. For saving him. I hit the gravel just beyond the field when I see Maddox step out from the barn with a tight expression. My insides flip, my nerves still rattled from this morning. I manage to keep my strides even, walking toward him without giving anything away. Before I can breach the driveway, Cooper, Ryder, and Clyde are barreling out from the field to my left. My brows scrunch just as a black Ford King Ranch pulls up in front of us. The logo on the driver side door tells me exactly who's in that truck.

Rocky Bernard

"What the fuck is he doing here?" Maddox glances at Ryder who stiffens his posture.

The door swings open, the only thing visible being a pointed alligator boot that hits the gravel. The door shuts, and a man with a purple wild rag tied around his neck, a crips suit jacket, and pressed black wrangler jeans strides across the open space. The gold pinky ring on his finger reflects off of the sunlight as he moves with an arrogance that's sickening. His posse climbs out behind him. Two men I don't recognize.

"Bernard." Ryder's voice is hard.

"Mayson." He dips his chin, then glances around. "Just thought I'd come by and check on my neighbor."

“That wasn’t necessary.” Cooper crosses his arms.

I’m a few steps away from Maddox, but I don’t miss the way he casually slides over to stand in front of me. Like he’s silently shielding me from the man who’s been nothing but a problem for this town.

He’s rich. Manipulative, and will do anything to get his way. Rocky has never lost a fight, and according to the rumors, most never make it out alive. He plays dirty, and we’ve made sure to never have any reason to play the game with him.

“Seems there’s not much left to work with.” Rocky leans to the side, spitting his tobacco on the ground next to Clyde’s boots.

Clyde bristles, but Rocky just shoots him a cocky smirk. “My offer still stands to take it off of your hands," he says to my brother.

My eyes whip to Ryder who stands up straight. “No thanks.”

I try to step forward, slipping around Maddox to get a better gage on the conversation, when his hand catches my wrist.

I lightly gasp, and it warrants the attention of the man currently participating in a stare down with my oldest brother. His dark eyes drop to my feet, then move slowly up my torso, before locking on my eyes.

“Little Ivy Mayson.” He lets his tongue out to wet his lips. “You’ve.... grown up.”

I narrow my eyes. Not missing the insinuation.

“If you’re in the market for a job, I’m in need of a new assistant. Someone I can work closely with.” He pauses, his eyes dropping to my chest. “Someone to handle my personal things.”

“Get back in your truck.”

This low command comes from Maddox, his grip still firm on my wrist.

Rocky smirks, his gaze dropping to where Maddox has a death grip on me.

"Easy, Sheppard."

Maddox moves me behind him, while Ryder and Cooper step in line with him, forming a barrier of cowboy hats and muscle.

"And if you want to keep both eyes, you'll keep them on her face next time, Bernard," Maddox adds.

My cheeks heat at the gruffness of his voice and the way he defends me spurs confusion.

"You heard him," Cooper says. "It's time for you to leave."

Ryder rolls his shoulders back, clearly ready to throw a punch if necessary.

Rocky cocks an eyebrow before spitting one more time in the dirt. "See you around boys."

Once he gets in his truck and drives off, I wait for the three men to face me. Once they turn, I hold out my arms. "What the hell was that?"

It's Ryder who actually answers me.

"He wants the ranch."

Chapter Twelve

Maddox

Rocky Bernard can get fucked.

I already don't care for the man, or the way he tries to bulldoze his way around town. The way he tries to threaten Emmett. Even Ryder and Cooper. It pisses me off. But *her.* He won't get fucking close.

"What do you mean he wants the ranch?" Ivy crosses her arms, her eyes narrowing on her siblings.

"He wants to buy the ranch. Add to all the other properties he's weaseled his way into in Mayson Ridge." Cooper reaches for a toothpick from his pocket and pops it in his mouth.

"Dad would never sell." Ivy waves her hand. "Why would he even think dad would consider it?"

Silence engulfs us, the only thing making noise is Dale, Cooper's ancient blue heeler who's deaf in one ear. He hobbles over, grunting his way around Cooper's boots.

"What are y'all not telling me?" Ivy asks, her voice growing firm.

"Do you think you even have a right to know?" Ryder shakes his head. "You just show back up and demand answers."

I can feel this about to turn ugly. Quick.

"I love this family!" Ivy croaks, her eyes misting with tears. "I know I haven't been here. I've been in school and things just got away from me but that doesn't mean I don't care." Her voice cracks, and I clench my fist.

I hate when she cries. I always have. It makes me want to say *fuck the consequences* and hold her in my arms until the tears no longer exist. My arms casting a shield to protect her from anything in this world that has the potential to make a single tear fall. I watch Cooper lift a brow at Ryder.

You really going to make her cry, man?

"Fuck, Ivy." Ryder sighs.

I know he can only give her the cold shoulder for so long.

Once she cries, he's done for. He won't admit it, but her leaving cut him deep, for different reasons than everyone else, but if he has a soft spot for anyone it's her and his mom.

Striding over he wraps an arm around her as she buries her face in his chest. "I'm sorry, okay?" She cries.

"Yeah. Me too." He pats her back a few times before she pulls away, swiping a tear.

"I don't really know how to say it other than to just say it, so." He pulls his hat off, running a hand over his hair. "The ranch is sort of in trouble."

"What do you mean trouble?" She sniffs.

"I mean, the finances aren't looking good. Haven't been for a while," he admits.

"Like we're going to lose this place, or it's just been a tough year?" She asks.

Ryder's silence must give her the answer because she closes her eyes. I'd known Emmett was strapped. The bills kept coming, the turn around taking longer, and the income dwindling. We also had a few hits last winter. But it wasn't my business to tell.

"And now this." She motions to the house.

"Yeah. Now this." Cooper shrugs. "I'm not sure if we can take this hit. Even with the insurance money."

"Do you know the specifics?" She places her hands on her hips. "Honestly, that's something that needs to be looked at immediately. We need to know what policy he has and if it's even updated."

Emmett was old school. He hated computers and did most of his stuff by hand. He typically kept most of the finances to himself. The only finances I have access to are the sale contracts on the breeding or the stock contracts for events.

"He's been using the office across from mine for about a year now. I'm sure if he has anything related to the ranch, it's in there," I offer.

"Ivy, I don't have a clue how dad keeps his things. He's always kept us at arm's length when it came to paperwork." Ryder drops his hat back on his head.

"Ryder, I'm a business major with a minor in accounting. I actually have a job handling the business side of a flower shop back in Atlanta. I have a good eye and if I can get my hands on any documents, it might make this situation less stressful. Dad isn't even awake yet, and pretty soon the fire department and the insurance companies will be calling. Mom has no idea, and especially with that slime ball coming around, we need to be on top of everything." Ivy nods, her eyes dancing over all of us.

"She's got my vote," Cooper says. "I don't have a fucking clue how to read an insurance policy."

"Not surprising since you barely graduated," Ryder mutters.

"Fuck off." Cooper flips him off. "I'm the creative type."

Cooper was too busy chasing bulls and buckle bunnies to actually show up for class. Dakota was the only reason he made it through.

"Shep." Ryder snags my attention. "Take her to the office. Might as well let her take a look. It can't hurt." Ryder turns to leave, then glances back over his shoulder. "Ivy."

"Yeah?" Her eyes look hopeful.

"I'm glad you're here." He pauses. "Just give me some time, yeah?"

She nods and tucks her hair behind her ears. "Ok."

Ryder heads back to the horses, then Cooper follows. I face Ivy, slipping back into the act. The one where I pretend breaking her heart didn't completely shatter my own.

"Come on. I'll walk you."

Chapter Thirteen

Ivy

I have papers and file folders scattered across my father's so-called desk. His *desk* concluded of two pieces of plywood stacked on top of some old feed barrels. It was so him, and absolutely dysfunctional. Majority of the things in the three tubs I found were receipts. Some going back to 1995, which was bordering the line of hoarding and not good record keeping. It was nearing eight o'clock and I hadn't found what I was looking for yet. Organization was not one of my father's best qualities and it might take me longer than expected to help them get their ducks in a row. Maddox had been across the hallway from me all evening. Silent and glaring. I don't know why he's so pissed at me. It's not like I broke into his cabin on purpose or that I'm the one who was so cruel the last time we spoke. That was all him, so if anyone has a right to be angry it's me.

His light flips off across the hallway, and I pretend I don't notice. I pretend I don't notice his lingering presence in the door frame either. I fumble through a box I have balanced on my thigh, not even looking at the pages. I'm hyper aware of his eyes on me.

"It's late." His deep voice fills the room, my skin tingling.

"So go to bed," I quip, before briefly glancing at him. "I'll grab my bag when I'm done here. Go crash at Cooper's."

"It's fine," he clips. "Just stay."

No, it's not fine. There is no way I can stay in the same house as him. According to the disaster that is before me, I'll be here a week or two. Not the couple of days I expected. I refuse to be in the next room if God forbid he brings a woman home. I'm not naïve. I grew up with two brothers and ranch hands my entire life. I know men. I know cowboys, and an empty bed isn't something they keep.

"I will be moving my stuff. It was a misunderstanding," I reiterate.

Being the stubborn ass he is, he takes a stride into the room. "You're not sleeping on Cooper's fucking sofa. It's not even a full size one. Your back will hurt."

I pause my fingers, my gaze drifting to his. To anyone else this would seem like someone telling you the couch is a piece of trash, and anyone would be uncomfortable on it. But it's that last line. *Your back will hurt.* I place the box down onto the plywood, my heart hammering inside of my chest. He's referring to my unfortunate accident. The one that has kept me off the back of a horse since I was seventeen. He knows how hard it was for me to sleep those first few months. How uncomfortable I can be sometimes. He's acting concerned, and that ignites a fire inside of me bigger than the one that just burned down my house.

"My back is fine." I straighten my shoulders. "I know what I can handle."

His jaw tics and if I'm not mistaken, he almost winces.

"I think it would be best if I stayed with Cooper." I step around the box, ready to call it a night and get as far away from him as possible. "I'm here to deal with family matters." I step up next to him, and dig the knife in a little further because I'm irritated that I'm still hurt after all this time. "Which you are not."

His hard eyes hold mine, and I can feel the heavy beat of my pulse. "Now, if you will excuse me. I have bags to move."

I make one quick step around him when my phone rings. I slip it out of the pocket of my dress, seeing *mom* flash across my screen.

I swipe, lifting the phone to my ear. "Mom? Everything ok?"

"He's awake," she breathes out through happy tears. "And he's asking for you."

I can feel my entire body stiffen, my lungs burning as I take a deep breath. "Ok. I'm on my way."

I end the call, turning to face Maddox. "He's awake."

He dips his chin, his legs already striding toward the door. "Let's go."

"Let's?" I flip the light off, following him out into the hall. "I can drive myself."

"It's dark now. That stretch of road is dangerous." He keeps talking, not even looking at me. "I'll drive you."

"That won't be necessary," I tell him, before I'm picking up my purse that I had tossed onto the entry table of the office.

His large palm presses against the door as he opens it for me. I ignore him, stalking through as I type out a text to my brothers.

I stop dead in my tracks when I get an immediate response.

Me: Dad is awake. I'm going up there.

Cooper: I'm already on my way. Ryder is already there. Maddox will drive you.

Me: I don't need him to drive me.

Cooper: He's driving you. Your eyes suck at night.

Me: I have glasses.

Cooper: Did you bring them?

I take a moment to reply, my teeth sinking into the side of my mouth.

Cooper: That's what I thought. You weren't wearing them last night. No night driving for you.

I swear they hover more than a stage five helicopter mom. You hit one deer and total a Ford F150 and all of a sudden you can't drive at night.

When I glance up, Maddox is holding the door open to his truck.

"Let's go. I don't have all night."

Chapter Fourteen

Maddox

My hands grip the steering wheel while I try to focus on not breathing through my nose. Her perfume is like sunshine and rain and it's fucking with my thought process. I knew the role I had to play. I knew it four years ago when I got too close. It wasn't her fault. She didn't do anything wrong; it was me. I crossed the line. Brady had been through enough, and sometimes I feel like we both turned our eyes away from his choices. Tried to give him the benefit of the doubt. Neither of us wanted to hurt him. She didn't want to break his heart and I didn't want to give him another reason to resent me. But that line had to be drawn, no matter how much I wished it didn't exist. I drew it in the sand that night and now I was here, and she was there. In the same fucking truck but a whole different galaxy.

I punch on the radio, keeping it at a decent enough volume that neither of us feel the obligation to make small talk. Just because she was back in Mayson Ridge, it didn't change anything. She still hated me, and I still deserved it. But my resolve is only so strong. I can handle a few days with her in my cabin. I like to think I'm a man of self-control. What kind of a dick would I be if I let her sleep on a shitty couch while there was a soft bed available knowing about her back issues. It would raise suspicion if I didn't at least try to convince her, and I wasn't aiming to draw any attention to us or our complicated past.

When we finally pull into the hospital, I park as close to the front as space will allow. She's out the door before I can make it to her side. I'm tempted to scold her. She knows the rules when riding in my truck and I may have been a prick at times, but I was a gentleman.

Her feet are quick, and her shoulders hunched as she walks through the automatic doors. I hadn't been in a hospital since the night I lost my father, but I shove it aside. This wasn't about my baggage; this was for her. For Emmett. I owed him a lot and the least I could do was make sure she gets to see him.

The elevator ride is just as tense as the drive. She kept her eyes away from me, her foot tapping a rapid beat against the floor.

When the doors slide open, she rushes out. I sigh before rubbing a hand over my face. My feet slide across the blue linoleum, but I halt when I see Ivy frozen at the edge of the waiting room. I slowly approach, hovering just behind her to give her a moment. As far as I know she hasn't seen Emmett in a while, and I can feel the anxiety rolling off of her.

After a few moments, I finally step up behind her.

"We can leave," I say quietly.

She swallows, giving me one curt shake of her head. "No." She clears her throat. "I need to do this."

Before I can press my palm to the small of her back like a complete fool, because it would only make this worse, she vaults forward, moving toward his room with determination. I follow closely, until she reaches the door. I stop, glancing back to the waiting room.

"I'll be out here." I hike a thumb over my shoulder.

I made it into the building. Going into that room is another story.

Her eyes meet mine, and a flash of empathy crosses them.

She knows.

"Okay. I won't be long." She disappears inside the room, while I disperse to a corner chair in the waiting area, trying to forget what my dad looked like laying in that same bed.

The second we get back to the cabin, Ivy heads straight to the spare bedroom. I hear some rustling before she emerges with two bags and a laptop.

"Ivy." I hold out my hands. "It's almost eleven. Just stay here."

"I appreciate the offer. But no thanks." She hikes one of the bags up. "I would rather stay with Cooper."

It shouldn't sting, but it does. Before she left Mayson Ridge there was a lot of unspoken words. Apologies that needed to be made on my part, but I never got the chance. I never got the chance to tell her I fucked up, so I took it as a sign. Me and her....it just creates more problems than solutions. It effects more than just the two of us and if

I've learned anything since my dad left this earth, it's not to be selfish. I can't be selfish, even though I want to. So damn bad.

"Ok." I move closer, reaching for her bags.

"I got it." She turns away.

"Ivy, there aren't any lights on the path to the barn. It's dark. It's summer and we have rattle snakes. Let me walk you and carry your bags."

She stares at me a moment before finally letting out a surrendering breath. "Fine."

I take both bags, opening the door and giving her enough space to walk through before snatching a flashlight by the door. Shining the light ahead, I watch her move, careful not to shine where she can't see.

"Be careful by this fence..." I begin.

But she interrupts by tossing her hands up. "I've lived here my entire life, Maddox. I think I know the way to the barn."

"Ivy." As soon as the word leaves my mouth, she stumbles, her flimsy shoe catching on a loose rock.

"Damn it," she hisses as her hands clench at her ankle.

The bags meet the dirt, and I'm crouched down in front of her before she can protest.

"Let me see."

"I'm fine," she hisses as she drops to her butt.

"Goldie," I say calmly.

She freezes, her eyes slowly drifting up to mine.

"Please let me see it?" I ask, my hand brushing along her calf.

Her breath hitches, but she masks her reaction, blinking her eyes. "It doesn't even hurt."

My palm wraps around where her hand is placed, and she winces. "You're a terrible liar. Have been since you were a kid."

She scoffs. "I am not. Remember when I got in trouble for stealing dad's gin?" She lifts a blonde eyebrow.

"Yeah. You got your ass ripped for two weeks about that." I can't help but grin at the memory.

"Well guess who fibbed?" She leans back on her palms, the movement hiking her dress up her thigh. I swallow, trying to avoid the smooth flesh.

"Me. It was actually Dakota, but I didn't want her to get in trouble. She sold the bottle to some old man in the trailer park so she would have lunch money for the week."

There's that golden heart.

"I never even told her that I got in trouble," she whispers next.

The silence hangs as my light shines down on her ankle that's already swelling. Without waiting for the response that I'm most likely going to ignore, I scoop her up in my arms and haul her back to my cabin.

Chapter Fifteen

Ivy

I would protest, but at this point what good would it do? Maddox deposits me on the kitchen counter, then snags a bandana from a small drawer. I watch him pull open the top door to the fridge, removing a handful of ice cubes before he wraps them up in the cloth.

"Here." He motions his hand for me to lift my foot.

I do, bracing my hands under my knee to keep it steady. His skilled hands remove my sandal, unhooking the clasp with ease. It spikes an irrational pang of jealousy. *I'm sure he's removed countless sandals off of women from the neighboring three counties.* He cups my heel and places the ice on the portion of my ankle that already looks bruised. I ignore the way his hands feel on my skin. The way he pretends to care. He doesn't. He was very clear on that the last time we were in a room alone together, so I don't really understand the reason for these theatrics.

"Thanks. I can take it from here." I clear my throat.

He ignores me. The opposite hand bracing on the countertop as he glances up at me.

"I'm sorry about the big house."

I blink as the unexpected lump in my throat forms. I didn't want this Maddox. The one in the white hat. The one who swoops in and wipes my tears. The one who makes everything *better.* No. I wanted the scowl. The rejection. It was easier to hate him that way. It was easier to be angry than hurt, and right now, I'm fragile. My world has been turned upside down in a matter of days, and now I'm sitting on his counter while he tends to my injury like some cowboy savior. Two days ago, he was the man who I vowed to never even speak to again if I didn't have to. But here we are, a breath apart, and he wants to act like he didn't use me and dispose me in the same breath all those years ago.

"Yeah, me too." Sliding his hand away; I maneuver myself down from the counter. "Thanks for the ice."

He steps back, his eyes still holding onto my every move. I can tell by his posture that he's not ready to cut this conversation short, but I am.

"Look Ivy, about what happened..." he starts, but I hold up a hand.

"Maddox, we don't have to hash out the past." I shrug a shoulder, doing my absolute best to give the illusion that what I'm saying is the God's honest truth.

"And if I want to?" He lifts a brow.

"There would be no point." I swipe my sandal from the counter. "What happened, happened. It's been years. Honestly, I haven't thought much about that night in a long time. I've been kind of busy."

He crosses his arms, the tic in his sharp jaw visible.

"It's not like I'm here for long anyway. We don't need to waste any time making things weird. I've moved on. So did you."

After my speech, I lift my chin, trying to control my breathing. If it wasn't for my pride I would fall flat on this dirty floor and cry.

He takes a slow step, his boots dragging across the wood, making the only sound in the cabin besides the warning bells going off inside of my head. His arms stay crossed, his eyes zeroed in on mine, as the final step brings him to stand directly in front of me. I hold my breath, my neck tilting back a fraction as he peers down at me. When he leans in, I inhale as his scent hits me with vengeance. His warmth fans across the junction of my shoulder, where my neck is bare from the spaghetti strap of my dress.

"You're a bad liar, Goldie." I squeeze my eyes shut, as he brushes past me, and I don't open them until I hear the click of his bedroom door.

Chapter Sixteen

Maddox

My hands rest in my pockets as I let my eyes trail over the bull pens. At one point in my life, I thought I'd be the man riding these machines. The one to make that glorious eight second ride, have my name displayed across the jumbotron with the crowd going wild. But it wasn't in the cards for me. I couldn't travel from rodeo to rodeo after dad died. My siblings needed me. My mom needed me, and so that dream was pushed aside, and it led to me dropping an idea in Emmett's ear. Instead of being the man on the bull, maybe I could be the one to provide the bull. Seeing as Ivy's cousin Parker Stillwater was becoming one of the top bull riders in the PBR, Emmett took interest in the business proposition and that interest led to the purchase of the Mayson Ranch's first bucking bull and its only grown from there.

Emmett entrusted me with this portion of the ranch, and I've never had more pride than when I look out over these magnificent creatures. We were lucky enough to start with a prime bull who could not only perform, but his bloodline gave us the ability to expand. To get into the breeding industry which is what has been the main source of income for the ranch the last couple of years. But even with the revenue from the contracts and the rodeos, the ranch is suffering, and Emmett's too fucking hardheaded to admit it.

I've already made notes on the white board of what the bulls need to be fed. Feeding these animals isn't just some oats dumped in a bucket. It's precise. It's specific to the bull, especially to the ones we use for breeding. This last year has been slower in terms of events, but we have a couple of places to hit later this season, and I have someone coming tomorrow to pay top dollar for some Havoc DNA.

Aiden and Hoss help me with the feeding, and they typically do most of it after I've laid out the diet. At first, I only allowed myself to do it. I didn't trust any of the ranch hands to not fuck up my operation. Even Ryder and Cooper want no part, but if I happen to be out of town, or for some reason can't be here, I need someone else who knows how to handle them correctly. Aiden has proved he's just as invested in these animals as Emmett and me. He's a hard worker and a damn good horseman. Hoss is just a kid, but he's eager to learn.

After I've made the notes for them, I head out of the bull barn and amble straight to the horse barn to begin my morning routine. Keeping a norm will help me sort shit out in my head. The main topic being the petite blonde who's sleeping under the same roof as me. The woman I haven't been able to rid from my psyche no matter how many beers I drink or how hard I work myself to the bone. She stays there. *Everywhere.* It's not my domain, it's Cooper's, but I have my reasons for my daily visits, and he doesn't ask any questions. I'm not sure whether he doesn't care, or he already knows the answer. Either way I appreciate his turning of a blind eye.

An hour later I'm about to retreat to my office when my phone rings. It's just after sunup now, barely seven o'clock.

"Hey ma," I answer.

"Morning." I can hear the yawn in her voice. "How's my boy?"

"Same as always." I press the phone between my ear and shoulder as I enter the office.

Millie Sheppard is a saint. A woman who spent her nights working at the Silver Ridge assisted living facility. She had the biggest heart, the kindest soul, and more patience than any human on this earth. Which is why I'd do anything for her. After all, I'm the reason she became a widow at the age of forty-six.

"Would you mind stopping by later today? That fire alarm in the hallway has been beeping for a week and it's driving me insane. I would change it but..."

"But nothing. I'll handle it." I shut the door behind me and flip on the lights.

She sighs. "Thank you."

She never has to thank me. I'm happy to do it. We all know Brady is never available to do anything she needs, and Laiken has her plate full with Trace. It leaves me.

"I'll be by after lunch," I tell her as I approach my office door.

"Ok. I'll get a few hours of sleep in. Love you."

"Love you." I end the call, but my steps slow when I see the light already on in Emmett's office.

I stop at the threshhold to see Ivy's cheek pressed against the plywood, her body resting on the old rusty office chair.

I step inside, waiting for her to move or to startle at my presence, but she doesn't budge. Black lashes touch her cheeks, her breathing even. She's sound asleep on a mound of documents. A part of me wants to wake her up just to drive home that she's not supposed to be walking on her ankle. But the other part of me, the part that would just rather let her rest after the recent events wins this round. Not wanting to wake her, I walk to my office, and lower down in my chair. My hand scrubs across my face, and when it drops to my thigh, I freeze. There it sits. Right on top of my desk calendar.

A wildflower.

Chapter Seventeen

Ivy

Why is my face wet? I blink open my eyes, my head snapping up when I see the plain taupe wall and not an actual bedroom. Drool is on the corner of my mouth, along with the insurance policy I finally found at exactly four eighteen this morning. I couldn't sleep. Not with everything on my mind. Not with my visit to the hospital last night. Dad was heavily medicated so he couldn't form a coherent sentence let alone hash out my disappearing act. So much was weighing on me. My father's health. My destroyed memories, and the man that was not even twenty feet across the hallway from me after magically developing a bedside manor. So, I got up, threw on whatever clothes I could find in my suitcase first and went back to digging through files. I finally found the golden ticket that was thankfully current and more than enough to rehabilitate this place. *At least I hoped.* I haven't exactly gotten to sort through the financials, but the close to one point two million that was securely stated on those documents would make a dent. That would be the next step after I talk with Cooper and Ryder.

Letting out a long breath, I wipe my mouth with the back of my hand and push to my feet. I could use a shower and some toothpaste at the moment. A flash from the catastrophe yesterday morning makes me wince and I shift my eyes to Maddox's office. *Empty.* My nerves ease slightly as I snatch up my phone and the documents before heading back to his cabin. My phone reads nine o'clock, along with a missed call from Dakota and a text from Merit.

Merit: Checking on you friend. Call me when you can.

My thumb moves to the call icon, and I bring it up to my ear as I enter the cabin, heading directly to the laundry room to grab a towel.

"Hey. How is everything?" Her soft voice flows into my ear.

"Fine," I lie, opening the dryer to find it empty.

Part of me is embarrassed. He folded the towels that fast? Like seeing me naked was traumatizing enough to fold laundry at midnight.

"Don't lie, Ivy," Merit scolds.

Maybe I am bad at it?

My boss wasn't like any other. She was my *friend* first, my boss second.

"It's a mess," I admit.

I make my way back to the guest room. I refuse to call it mine and grab a change of clothes.

"Take all the time you need."

Merit was the most empathic person I'd ever met. She reminded me of Laiken in that way. She had been my first real friend in Georgia, and even though I haven't ever told her about my family issues, she knew about Maddox. One night with a few too many wine spritzers and a bad date that I refused to kiss, I spilled my guts. It was the first time I'd talked about my feelings for him out in the open. I hadn't even told Dakota. I felt like she'd be keeping secrets from Laiken, and I know firsthand how that felt. I didn't want to put her in that place.

"It may be a week or two. I can do all of my work from my laptop, so no worries there."

"I'm not worried about work." I can hear the jingle of the shop door opening in the background. "I'm just worried about you. Have you seen him?"

I blow out a breath. "Yeah. I've seen him."

Before I can elaborate, I hear the jingle again. "Sorry, Ivy. Alanzo just walked in. I'll call you later to check in."

She hangs up quickly before I can respond, and that uneasy feeling strikes in my gut. It always did when Alanzo came into the shop. He's Merit's boyfriend, and even though he's never done anything *wrong*, he always gave me a bad vibe. But who was I to give dating advice? I had only been on a total of three dates in the last three years. One which ended with me attempting to have sex in the back seat of a Dodge Durango. When I panicked halfway to second base, I was dropped off at my apartment and I never heard from him again. Which was fine. It wasn't like I was in love with *Josh*. He was everything Maddox wasn't, and it was the only reason I swiped right. Then I ended up spending my evening crying in the shower over the fact that I almost gave a part of myself, the small part that in my heart only belonged to one man, to a complete stranger.

Putting aside my thoughts, I escape to the bathroom and start the shower. When I glance out the window, my eyes catch on a familiar figure. The one walking toward the barn with a stride I could pick out of any crowd. It took almost all of my strength, but I tore my eyes away. Even now, it still hurt to look at him. And I'd love to know when that feeling will finally go away.

Chapter Eighteen

Ivy

The Mayson Jar is bubbling with the lunch rush as I enter the resturaunt. I'm meeting Cooper and Ryder to go over the information I found and let them know they could breathe easy. At least we had something to fall back on once the fire chief is finished with his report. I wasn't sure how long it would take the insurance company to pay out, so I still wanted to dig through the finances as long as dad and mom were ok with it.

After Fern leads me to a table across from the bar, she drops some menus down and fortunately doesn't question me today.

"Hey sugar," Penelope calls from the kitchen door.

I wave as she winks and disappears with an empty tray balancing on her shoulder. When I face forward, I'm met with a pair of light brown eyes.

Brady.

With a wide smile he strides over, sliding into the booth across from me. "Eating alone?"

I grab a menu and flip it open. "Not today. Just waiting on Coop and Ryder."

He nods and I don't miss the way his eyes access me. It's not heated. It's not really even sexual, it's more of a look from a long-lost friend. Like he's trying to see what's changed. "I'm glad you're back."

I shake my head. "I'm not back, Brady. Just here until we get everything sorted."

"How's your dad?" He asks.

"He's ok. I plan on stopping by after this." I place the menu down and fold my hands together. "Do you know when the fire chief plans to come out?"

His fingers drum against the table, a move he's absent mindedly done since we were kids. "Not sure. I think he mentioned sending Nixon out."

Warren Nixon was the fire captain and had been since I was thirteen. "They'll get it all taken care of."

"Thanks. I appreciate it." My hand moves to tuck my hair behind my ear. "The last couple of days have been kind of hectic."

Brady reaches out, his palm covering my hand that still rests on the plastic menu. "I'm really sorry, Ivy."

His words are sincere, and it's nice to hear them. It's clear that Brady has come a long way, and I was proud of him. I've always wanted the best for him. Regardless of our relationship status.

"Thank you," I whisper as my eyes are summoned to the jingle coming from the door that just opened, bringing in the sunshine and a cowboy hat.

It didn't take long for my gaze to lock with the pair of hazel eyes hidden beneath the brim. Maddox's stare holds mine only for a second, before they dip to Brady's hand on mine.

Those eyes then veer over to the bar and I instinctively tug my hand away. Brady must have followed my line of sight, because he glances over his shoulder, calling for Maddox with a wave. Maddox briefly lifts his hand in greeting before taking a seat at the bar.

"Need a drink?" He asks.

"Sure." I smile weakly, my heart skipping a beat as I peer over at Maddox's back.

"Be right back." Brady winks, then hustles to the bar, while I use his absence to take in a solid breath.

The last thing I want is to give my ex any ill illusions. But right now, for some idiotic reason, I'm only worried about the illusions his older brother has.

Chapter Nineteen

Maddox

"Hey man." Brady slaps a hand on my shoulder.

"Hey." I have to put forth effort to not sound like a jealous asshole.

He nods at Shorty, the bartender who's shamelessly flirting with the reverend's wife.

"Can I get two cokes?" Brady calls. "One to go please."

My stomach knots.

When Shorty places the drinks down, Brady leans on his elbow. "Can you put two cherries in this one?"

"Since when do you drink cherry coke?" I nudge him, trying to go back in time where we ribbed each other, not landed punches.

"It's for Ivy." He hikes a thumb in her direction.

I've always been good at choosing my words, but for some reason, I choose that exact moment to let the words fly from my mouth with more accusation than I intended. "Why? She hates cherries."

Brady frowns. "Ivy? No, she doesn't."

"Yes, she does." I take a gulp of the ice water in front of me. "She used to pick the cherries off of her Sundays."

Brady tilts his head, like he's trying to recall the memories.

Anger slowly begins to build. It always does when I think back to how he was with her. How the fuck did he not know she hates cherries? He dated her for four years. Known her as long as I have.

"Huh." He shrugs. "I don't remember that."

Of course he doesn't.

And these are the times I find myself frustrated with my brother. He never remembers anything unless it involves himself. Mom's birthday. Laiken's graduation. Hell, he wasn't even in town when Trace was born and didn't see him until he was almost a month old.

And like the jealous asshole I am, I nod my head in the direction of the booth that houses my girl. "Lunch date?"

He chuckles. "Nah, she's waiting on Cooper and Ryder." His eyes volley over to her. "Not sure she'd agree to a date after how things went down with us."

I didn't even realize I was holding my breath until I let it out. I needed to get my shit together. I had no claim over her. Never have. But the mere thought of his hand over hers makes my stomach sour and my muscles tense.

"I have to get back to the station. Just came to pick up lunch." He smacks my shoulder again. "Don't forget, we still have plans for those beers."

He slides the drinks from the bar, dropping Ivy hers before he saunters out the door.

Cooper and Ryder walk in not seconds later, shooting me a wave as they weave through the tables and over to their sister. I fight like hell to keep my attention on the flat screen above the bar. The one playing Urban Cowboy, but I can't help it. It's like this invisible string that's always pulled me to her. I glance over my shoulder, and when I do, I can't help but let my lip tilt in an arrogant smirk. Ivy dips her fingers into her coke before tossing the cherries out onto a napkin.

She hates cherries.

Why does that small fact make me feel like she's mine?

Chapter Twenty

Ivy

Six years ago

Two hours. He's two hours late.

"Maybe he had car trouble?" My mom offers as she gives me a pitiful glance.

I pace back across the wooden planks, the heels of my boots thudding beneath the prom dress I spent two months searching for.

"He's not coming." The words are bitter on my tongue but true.

I should have expected it by now. I've given Brady the benefit of the doubt for too long. Forgiven him too many times.

"I'm sorry, sweetheart." Mom sighs, walking to me with open arms. "You can still go to prom. It's senior year. You can't miss it."

Her warm embrace wraps around me, and I feel less like strangling a tall cowboy who's proved he has zero respect for me. I know I should have ended it months ago, truthfully even years. Again, my own fault. But as I stand here all dressed up, waiting on my date that chose not to show, I have nothing left to give.

"It's fine." I wave a hand.

I refuse to walk into that gymnasium alone and confirm what everyone else already knows. What the whole town will be talking about.

"I wasn't all that excited to go anyway," I lie.

I can tell by her pursed lips she doesn't believe me, but instead of pushing, she kisses my temple.

"Please don't tell dad." I groan. "He'll probably show up at Millie's with a shotgun."

She laughs. "I won't tell. He and your brothers wont' be back until tomorrow, so you can avoid an interrogation."

"Thanks."

Her fingers tuck a blonde curl behind my ear. "You want any company?"

I shrug a shoulder. "Not really."

With a gentle touch to my cheek, she leaves me alone and without even removing my dress, I slip out to the barn. The smell of fresh hay and horses puts my nerves at ease as I walk up to Sugarfoot's stall. "Hey there girl."

Dipping my hand into the cubby next to me, I pull out a few treats.

"He didn't show up." I hold out my hand as she nibbles her lips along my fingers. "Truth is I'm not upset that he stood me up. I'm upset that I'm missing time with my friends."

She takes the treat, and I smooth my hand up her nose. "What does that mean?"

You know what it means, Ivy. Admit it's over.

With a sigh, I rest my chin on the gate, my gaze fixed on the night sky beyond her pen.

"Shouldn't you be at prom?"

My head turns toward the deep voice that flows from behind me. Maddox stands in the doorway, a fresh pearl snap covering his chest, along with a pair of clean wranglers.

"I would be if your brother bothered to show up." I push away from the gate.

I watch the way his eyes move over me, before they meet mine again.

He clears his throat. "You...you look gorgeous."

"Thanks." I can feel the blush in my cheeks along with the skipping beats of my heart.

"He didn't show?" He asks, his feet gravitating toward me.

"What's new, right?" I quip.

He shakes his head, before he slips off his hat and runs his fingers through his dark hair. I've noticed he does this when he's frustrated.

"It's bullshit, Ivy," he scoffs.

"I know," I answer.

He stops in front of me, his hand lifting to my hair, but he pulls it back at the last second, his brows furrowing. He doesn't speak for a moment before asking.

"You want to go somewhere?"

Yes. Anywhere with you.

The single thought flashes across my brain, and my heart stutters.

"The ridge?" I offer.

With a sharp nod he turns on his heel, and even though a slither of guilt works its way into my chest, I ignore it and follow.

"Can you believe this view?" I ask, gazing up at the stars.

The ridge at the back of the ranch is one of my favorite places. Besides the flower field, or the barn, it's where I come to think. To just absorb the silence when I feel like I can't hear my own thoughts.

"It's fucking beautiful," he says next to me.

I smile, but when I glance at him, he's not looking up at the stars, he's looking at me.

My skin tingles under his gaze, my hands clenching the fabric of my dress. This feels dangerous. It feels wrong. It feels wrong to admit I feel more at ease with him than I do with anyone else.

To break whatever moment is quickly forming, I blurt. "All I really wanted to do tonight was dance."

He searches my face, before he hops off of the tailgate of his truck. Fishing his phone from his pocket, he thumbs the screen before placing it down on the side.

He offers me an open palm. "Then let's dance."

"Maddox." I laugh, trying to ease the racing of my heart. "You don't have to."

"I said let's dance, Goldie."

Goldie. That's the first time he's ever called me that.

Without another intrusive thought, I slip my hand in his as he guides me down to the ground. My boots hit the dirt; the hem of my dress doing the same. He tugs me to his chest, his hand settling on the small of my back. The music begins to flow from the small speaker on his phone, filling the empty space with a beautiful melody. George Strait's The Man in Love with You *plays softly as we move together beneath the sky. And for the very first time, I allow myself only a fraction of a second to wonder what it would be like to be loved by Maddox Sheppard.*

Chapter Twenty-One

Ivy

"So, this is good right?" Cooper aims his question at Ryder who doesn't show a flicker of emotion. "Yeah. I mean, thankfully it isn't expired."

Cooper blows out a breath, his blue eyes releasing the anxiety that's been held there since I arrived. "So, we can save it."

"I would like to say yes, but I need to do some research before we know how deep the ranch is." I smile as Judith; our waitress pours me a fresh cup of coke. One without cherries. I swear, for a man I've known since I was five he has absolutely no idea who I am. But he's at least trying, and I don't want to ruin his progress, so I accepted the drink and waited until he left to trash them.

"We should talk to dad," Ryder says. "He'll get pissed if we snoop without his approval."

I nod, knowing damn well he won't question me. He wants me to play my role, he'll have to play his. Someone that cooperates will be a foreign feeling for him, but tough shit. The ranch is on the line.

"I agree." Cooper whips out a toothpick. "Might as well do it now."

"That's fine." Ryder shrugs. "Clyde has the ranch covered for the next couple of hours."

I take a big gulp of my drink, then drop it back to the table. "Then let's get this over with."

Twenty minutes later we are surrounding my father's hospital bed. He's awake, our eyes connected for the first time in years.

"Ivy girl." His voice is hoarse as he adjusts the oxygen tube in his nose.

"Dad." I smile, because despite everything, it's good to see him awake. Breathing.

He coughs, his hand coming to his chest with a pained expression. My mom stands, adjusting his pillow so he can sit up better. Clear his airway.

"Thank you, sweetheart," he rasps, and mom places a kiss on his temple.

I feel the twist in my stomach, but I ignore it as he reaches his hand out for me.

With all eyes on me, I take it, not wanting to raise questions. I place mine in his and relief flashes in his red rimmed eyes. He clears his throat, knowing that when all of us are together at one time, it usually means we're up to something.

"What's going on?" My mother settles back in the chair next to his bed. "You look serious, Cooper."

Which is a rare occasion.

"They told me about the ranch," I blurt, causing dad's hand to squeeze against mine.

"What about the ranch. The fire?" Mom's brow furrows. "What are they talking about, Emmett?"

"Ruthie..." he coughs again before he curses low under his breath.

"How bad is it, dad?" I ask.

His eyes hold mine, while I straighten my spine. I can tell by his hesitation mom is the only one in this room who doesn't know. Seems not much has changed. He still hides the truth to *protect* her.

"The fire on top of everything else...." His hand trembles as he removes it from mine, then strokes his greying beard.

He always did this when he was thinking.

"I found the insurance policy. It's a generous amount. Should be plenty to rebuild the house, but as far as how deep in the red we are with the finances, I don't know how far the money will stretch. With you in here, that leaves us to help line things up. I'm just trying to help, dad," I offer gently.

He nods, his eyes veering to my mom. "I'm sorry, Ruthie. I didn't want you to worry."

"Hush. Just tell them," she urges.

"I've been able to keep up payroll. But with the last couple of droughts, and the head we lost last winter, along with feed prices going up, we got behind. We're barely paying the bills."

"How does Rocky know?" Ryder asks from the corner he's perched in.

Dad's face hardens. "Did he show up? That greedy bastard."

His monitors start beeping, indicating a rise in his heart rate.

"Emmett." Mom stands. "You need to breathe."

He takes a deep breath, releasing another harsh cough. Once he calms, he rests his head back on the pillow.

"How would he know, dad?" Cooper asks next. "I know he's always wanted the ranch, but he's been like a vulture the last couple of years."

Dad's sigh is audible as he closes his eyes. "Back taxes."

"Taxes?" I glance at Ryder.

"How much?" Ryder asks

"Son..."

"How much?" It's my turn to ask.

"Fifty grand," he admits.

"Fuck," Ryder scoffs.

"Language," mom scolds before facing my father. "Fifty grand, Emmett?"

"I know." He shakes his head. "It's my responsibility. It's not your burden."

"It's our ranch, dad. We all carry the burden," Cooper says.

"It's public record. That's how he knows." I can practically hear the growl in Ryder's voice.

Fantastic. How long before anyone else finds out?

"Ok. Dad, I need to know where you keep your files. I need everything."

He winces as he scoots up in the bed. "Most of my stuff is kept in the office. But I keep some of my receipts and invoices in the black binder. It's in my truck."

"Thank you." I reach for his hand again. "I will do my best. I'll comb through it all. We'll figure this out. You just focus on getting out of here."

I give my speech before I'm up on my feet. I can see by his eyes he wants to talk. To say more, but right now I'm not ready. I'm not ready to reopen that old wound. So, with my promise to figure it out, we leave the hospital, and I keep my mind focused on one thing. *The Mayson Legacy.*

Chapter Twenty-Two

Maddox

"Ok, I'm done." I drop my palms onto the couch, my arms burning from shaking Trace's makeshift bull that's set up in my mother's living room.

"One more. Pleeaase," he begs.

"It's bath time, mister." My sister walks into the living room, bending down to pick up his rope and spurs. "You're filthy. You need to get clean before super."

"But mom...."

"No buts. Go." She points.

His arms cross. "You ruin all the fun."

"Trace." My voice is stern, and he knows I mean business.

"Yes ma'am," he finally mumbles before he holds out his fist and I tap it with mine.

"Bye Uncle Mads."

"Later kid." I ruffle his hair when he walks by.

Laiken sighs and leans against the door frame. Pushing to my feet, I approach her and tug her in for a hug.

"You're doing a good job, Laik."

"Am I?" She pulls away, placing the items in her hand into the box full of farm animal figurines that's tucked in the corner. "I'm a twenty-five-year-old single mom who still lives with her mother. And apparently, I'm no fun."

I chuckle. "You're a badass mom, who worked hard to become a physical therapist and you're saving for your future."

Laiken has a bad habit of always thinking she's screwing up. She doesn't see the things she's accomplished.

"Yeah, if it wasn't for that scholarship I wouldn't have that degree." She stuffs her hands into the pockets of her purple scrubs.

"I'm proud of you," I tell her as her eyes mist over. "Dad would be proud of you."

She nods. "I know." She steps to me again. "Thanks, Mads."

I press a quick kiss to her hair as mom bounds down the stairs.

"I'm off." She clasps her favorite silver necklace around her neck.

"I fixed the fire alarm, and your AC filter is changed as well," I tell her.

"You're going to make some woman a fine handy man one day." She pushes up on the toes of her sneakers and plants a kiss on my cheek.

"How's Ivy? The boys? I talked to Ruthie yesterday. She said Emmett is doing better."

"They're fine. Taking it one day at a time."

She pats my shoulder. "Be safe. Love you both."

She rushes out, just as Trace bellows from upstairs. "Mom! Hurry! There's something weird under my toodle!"

A laugh barks from my chest as Laiken groans. "God had to give me a boy, didn't he?"

With my laugh still shaking my shoulders, I leave my sister to deal with the anatomy questions and climb in my truck.

Walking into the cabin, I go straight to the pantry and grab a can of ravioli. As a man, I don't need much. Food, sleep, a release every now and then, and this ranch. I'm simple. Which is why I use the handheld can opener to pop off the top and grab a spoon from the drawer to begin eating my dinner.

I dip into the can, about to wrap my lips around the square noodle of cheese when I hear a gasp from behind me.

I spin around to see Ivy at the threshold of the kitchen. Her hair that was down earlier is tied into a knot on top of her head, her legs bare beneath some cotton shorts. A sorry excuse for a tank top is covering her torso. She's barefoot, her white painted toenails the brightest thing in this cabin apart from her green eyes.

"Maddox. That's disgusting."

"What?" I look down at the spoon. "It's Chef Boyardee."

"It's cold." She grimaces.

"And?" I lift a brow while purposely keeping eye contact as I place the spoonful in my mouth.

"I don't understand men," she scoffs. "Give me that."

With one swift move she plucks it from my hand and drops it in the trashcan next to the fridge. "I'll cook something."

Cook something? With what? I haven't been to the store in two weeks.

She reaches for the fridge, and opens it, revealing fully stocked shelves. I frown and she notices.

"I went to the store. If I'm going to be stuck here for the next couple of weeks, I'd rather not starve."

"Thanks?" It comes out as a question.

I know she would rather be anywhere else. She hates me, and I have no one to blame but myself. But even though she despises me with every fiber of her being, here she is about to cook me dinner. Because Ivy Mayson is as good as fucking gold.

Chapter Twenty-Three

Maddox

Five years ago

After spending all day mending the fence between the Mayson Ranch and the Double B Ranch, I'm exhausted. Even after a grueling day, I was conned into spending an unreasonable number of hours at poker night in the bunk house until Clyde took all of my fucking money. It's almost one in the morning and the only thing calling my name is my bed. I toss my phone down on my dresser, about to flip off the light when a streak of blonde hair flashes past my bedroom window. There's only one blonde haired beauty that would be roaming around this time of night.

Peering out the glass, I see Ivy practically sprinting across the pasture to the tank. I curse under my breath when I spot the vodka bottle hanging from her fingers.

My legs are carrying me across the room in less than a second, my jeans zipped, and a t-shirt over my head next. I've learned that when Ivy drinks, she's usually upset. Which isn't often, and I'm not sure what shit my brother has pulled this time.

Five minutes later I've made it down to the tank in the pasture behind the barns. Ivy stands at the edge in nothing but her underwear and bra. I avert my eyes, trying not to notice the way the cheeks of her ass peek out from beneath the blue lace material.

"Ivy," I call as I climb out of the side by side. My tone is borderline angry. Which I am. Not with her. With the circumstances.

She glances over her shoulder. "Wanna swim with me?"

No. I need to stay as far away as humanly possible.

"No." I scrub a hand over my face as she wades out into the water.

"Fine. Then go home." Step by step she walks into the water, and as if my own damn limbs can't follow my brain's response, I feel my fingers flip open the button of my jeans.

Once I'm down to my boxers, I'm following her out into the water like a damn magnet.

She dips her head back, wetting her golden strands before she spins to face me.

Her eyes are glassy, and red rimmed. She's been crying. I grit my teeth, refraining from wrapping her in my arms and demanding to know who made her cry. Like I don't already know.

"What happened?" I ask, my slow movements causing the water to slosh up against my navel.

"It's over," she breathes out.

"Over?"

She opens her eyes, a tear falling. "Brady. I..." she runs her hands over the ripples in the water. "I spotted his truck in the parking lot at the rodeo grounds. He told me he had to work for Claude this evening. I just had a feeling, you know?"

Fuck.

"My feeling was correct." She lets out a humorless laugh. "He was balls deep inside some brunet in the back seat."

My chest burns. My hands itching to touch her. My words threatening to spill out that I'd never put her through that. I'd never hurt her like he has.

"I'm sorry, darlin" I tell her. "I'm sorry he hurt you."

She shakes her head with tears steadily falling. "That's the thing, Maddox."

My hands twitch. God, why do I love when she says my name?

"I'm not hurt." She peers up at the sky before meeting my eyes. "I'm relieved."

I take a step closer. Damn these feet.

"I'm relieved that I don't have to be the one to break his heart. I don't have to tell him the truth."

"And what's the truth?" I'm standing right in front of her now. One more lazy slide of my feet against this thick mud and my chest would brush hers.

"That I don't love him that way," she whispers. "Not the way that I...." She trails off and paddles back.

The way she what? My chest tightens as her hands come to her temples.

"I don't feel good." She stumbles and my arms shoot out to steady her. Another stumble has her falling into my chest.

"How much did you drink?" I ask, wrapping my arm around her waist.

Her answer slices right through me. "Enough to make the guilt go away."

I haul her to me, then cradle her against my bare skin, before I'm carrying her to the ATV.

When she passes out against my shoulder on the way back to the cabin, I carry her inside. A better man would put her on the couch. Cover her with a blanket and climb in his own bed. But I never said I was a better man. So, I place her in the spot next to where I sleep then lay down next to her. I stare up at the ceiling with my hands secured behind my head, listening to her soft breaths. Then I do something I've never done before. I roll over, tugging her close so my heartbeat rests against her spine. Then I whisper my confessions. Even though she won't hear a single word.

I won't let anyone ever hurt you again.

I've wanted to hold you like this for so long.

I can't breathe when you walk into the room.

Am I a bad guy for wanting you? When you didn't belong to me?

Chapter Twenty-Four

Ivy

I stare at the figure written in red ink on the sheet of paper in front of me. According to my calculations, the insurance money should be enough to pay the back taxes, rebuild the big house, and replace what we've lost with some left over to put in a savings account for emergencies only. I sink back into the old leather chair, somewhat relieved that we still have a fighting chance. Relieved that we can tell Rocky Bernard to kiss our ass, but I'm still nervous with how much time it will take for the information to go through the channels of authority. It could be weeks, or months, and until that money is in our possession, we still have bills to pay and employees to keep. It's not like the world stops turning when a tragedy hits.

Voices coming down the hallway of the office catches my attention, while I watch a man, and a woman enter Maddox's office across the hall. After I made dinner last night, I filled my plate then ate in my room. Alone. I was halfway through making lasagna soup when I realized I was doing it again. *Being nice.* Why I couldn't channel my inner Dakota and tell Maddox to fuck off and fend for himself is beyond me. So instead of sitting and forcing small talk like he didn't once humiliate me to my core, I made the announcement that dinner was ready then escaped to the only place I could breathe. *Away from him.*

"I've had my eye on that bull for months," the man says as he shakes Maddox's hand.

I have a clear view into his office, and I watch the man who must be in his early fifties adjust his straw cowboy hat before he braces his hands on his hips.

"He's top of the line. You won't find a better bloodline than his." Maddox takes a seat in his chair, his eyes meeting mine before the woman speaks.

"We are so grateful we found you. We don't want to deal with anyone but you," she practically purrs.

I roll my eyes as the bottled blonde with a skirt that's not exactly in her age category cocks a hip out against his desk.

The man chuckles, his gut moving along with the rhythm. He screams old money which has to be the only reason his *wife* is so enthusiastic.

"Mind if I take a look?" The man asks.

Maddox nods. "Absolutely."

He goes to stand, but the man holds up a chubby palm. "No need. I see where he's pinned. Daphne can square away the payment with you while I look him over."

"Sure thing. Aiden has your sample. He's bringing it from the breeding barn." Maddox relaxes back in his chair as *Daphne* beams with delight.

I pick up a pen, pretending to be focused on the documents in front of me, and not the cougar whose claws came out as soon as her husband left the room.

She plucks a check from her Louis Vuitton purse and flips her long hair. "You got a pen, sugar?"

Sugar?

Maddox smirks. "Yes ma'am."

I glance up to see her stand from the chair, bending at the waist as she grips the pen, then begins writing the check. I know her cleavage has to be on full display because the double Ds were barely contained beneath her silk top when she walked in.

My grip strangles the plastic in my hand, and I slide my eyes away from her to Maddox. Who's staring directly at me.

Shit.

I clear my throat, and pick up the papers, stacking them together before I place them neatly in a new folder. I hope the jealously wasn't plastered across my face. I don't even know why I'm jealous. Why would I want his attention? It's not like it means anything. I've learned that from experience.

I make the grand mistake of looking across the hall again. Only this time, *Daphne* has her mini skirt covered ass perched on the edge of his desk with her legs crossed as she giggles.

Fucking giggles.

He joins in, barking out a laugh.

I stand abruptly, my holder of pens crashing to the ground with my sudden movement. I fall to my knees, raking the pens into a pile while I close my eyes.

Can I be any more obvious?

Low voices are in the background, but I block them out as I clean up the floor. I'm reaching for the last pen when a large tanned hand snags it from the concrete. I glance up to see Maddox crouched in front of me, twisting the pen between his fingers.

"Everything ok in here, Goldie?"

Goldie.

My breath hitches and a flock of birds take flight in my belly at the nickname he keeps insisting on using.

"All good." I reach for the pen, but he yanks his hand back.

"You sure?"

I let out a huff. "Yes." I push to my feet. "Go back to your meeting. Looks like you were about to get a happy ending."

I want to die the second the words leave my lips. My cheeks flush and the asshole in front of me curls his lip into that sexy smirk that I have come to loathe.

"Does that bother you?' He tilts his head.

I scoff. "Why on earth would that bother me? The only thing *bothering* me is the fact you conduct your *extracurriculars* on this ranch during business hours and with married clients for that matter."

That's good Ivy. It's about business. The ranch. Adultery. Not your fragile heart mangled by the cowboy who is now full-on grinning.

"I don't mix business with pleasure," he says, holding out the pen for me.

I snatch it, my fingers brushing along his rough skin as I do. Tingles spread up my arm, and I don't miss the way his grin falters.

Did he feel it too?

I clear my throat just as Cooper steps into the doorway of the office. "Hey guys. Fire captain is here."

Thank God. Maybe he can put this fire out for me. It's been burning too long for Maddox Sheppard.

Chapter Twenty-Five

Maddox

Warren Nixon tucks his clipboard under his arm, then extends his hand to me. "Maddox."

I take it, before he moves his eyes to Ivy. "Good to see you, Ivy." He opens an arm as she steps up to him for a side hug that's completely innocent.

But that innocence doesn't stop the wave of possessiveness crawling inside of my skin when his hand brushes against her back. *You got some nerve, Shep.*

"Hey Warren. Thanks for coming out." She keeps her gaze averted from mine, and I'm even more convinced now that everything she said the other night was a lie. She wants to seem indifferent, but she was jealous in the office. It was written all over her pretty face and it had me feeling some sort of way.

"It would probably be easier for you to take the side by side. Getting through with a truck will be a bitch." Cooper leans against the door of his pickup.

"That's fine." Warren pulls his clipboard out. "It might take me a while given the amount that was damaged. But I'll find the source. It'll take me a couple of days to do my official report, but I'll have something by at least tomorrow or the next day."

Cooper nods, tossing him the keys before he steps over to Ivy. "You look tired."

"Is that code for you look like shit?" She rolls her eyes.

"No. It's code for you're spending too much time in dad's office." Cooper drapes an arm over her shoulder. "Why don't you get some fresh air."

"I don't need fresh air. I need all of this to be settled so I can go back to my normal life."

I feel a sharp pinch in my chest at her words.

"Well fuck me, Ivy." Cooper removes his arm. "I'm sorry this is so inconvenient for you."

"That's not what I meant, and you know it." She crosses her arms. "I just meant I want everyone healthy, and the ranch to be in the green. Just normal."

He sighs and runs a hand over his jaw. "I know." He glances at me. "Sorry. All this shit is getting to me too." He looks back to Ivy. "Why don't you take Sugarfoot out?"

The look on her face could ice out the bravest of warriors. "Cooper. You know I don't ride anymore."

"Why not?" He presses.

"You know why." She tosses her hands up.

"You know how many times I've been bucked off of a horse?" He questions.

"Twelve," I insert casually.

He glares at me. "Eleven."

"Man up, Cooper. That pony bucked your ass off." I chuckle.

"Tater Tot?" Ivy gapes.

"The one and only." I grin.

"Both of you can kiss my ass." Cooper rips open his door. "Now if you will excuse me, I've got to go pick up Dakota."

"What happened?" Ivy asks, her face growing serious.

"Her dad called her last night."

We fall silent, all knowing what that means.

"Tell her to call me if she needs me." Ivy softens. "I hate that he still gets to her."

"Yeah. Fucking piece of shit." Cooper spits. "He better be glad he's behind bars."

Cooper climbs in his truck before hollering out the open window. "I mean it, Ivy. We can't do anything until the report comes back. Relax. Enjoy being home."

Ivy waves a hand dismissively, but since going the easy route and ignoring her isn't something I'm capable of, an idea is already forming in my head. I know exactly what she needs.

Chapter Twenty-Six

Ivy

I wrap my hands around the ceramic coffee mug, letting the warmth settle against my palms as I stroll to the barn. It's already early afternoon, but as tired as I am, I'm going to need an obscene amount of caffeine to keep me lucid. I knew Cooper was right. I had a tendency to fixate on things until I had a raging headache or mettled into the insomnia territory. Plus, it would keep me away from Maddox and I could try to get myself under control. *Jealousy? Really, Ivy?*

I needed some time with Sugarfoot. I believe all the things that have been said about horses and therapy. I'd rather spend two hours with an equine therapist over a live human any day of the week. You can't describe it unless you've experienced it, and it does quite literally cause pain to my heart living with the fact I can't even get over my own fears to ride her again. Take her on the trials she loved so much.

The first thing I notice when I enter the barn is the new feeding trays, but then I lift my eyes, and skid to a stop.

"Hey," Maddox says over his shoulder as he runs a brush through Sugarfoot's long mane.

"What are you doing?" I narrow my eyes.

"What I do every day." He shrugs a shoulder.

Every day?

"Tend to the horses? I thought that was Cooper's job." I take a sip of coffee.

He keeps brushing with one hand, slipping a treat to her mouth with the other. "It is." He glances at me with those devastatingly beautiful eyes. I wonder how many hearts have stopped mid beat because of them. "But *I* take care of her."

My heart thuds. Then it flutters.

Damn him.

"Why?" I question.

"Because she's important to you." His answer is so simple, and he stops brushing long enough to face me. His next statement makes my throat burn. "And you're important to me."

His eyes cast down to my sandals. "You might want to change your shoes."

"What's wrong with these?" I lift my feet one at a time.

He smirks. "We're riding today."

I squeeze the cup in my hand on instinct. The word *riding* causing that familiar fear to resurface. He's not asking. "Maddox, no. I haven't ridden since I..."

"Since you got hurt. I know." He places the brush down on the bench beside Sugarfoot's stall. "You know it wasn't her fault. That rattlesnake was underneath her."

"I know." My voice strains.

Logically I know that. It was a freak accident. But I haven't been able to get back on. I still love her. She's still my horse. I just haven't been able to ride again without a panic attack.

"I know you're struggling with a lot of things right now." His dusty boots bring him closer. "And I know you feel like you can't trust anyone here. Obviously or you wouldn't have left, but you can trust her." He points back to the beautiful paint horse. "And I'd like to start building trust back with us. If you'll let me."

My heart can't take it. I flicker my eyes to Sugarfoot, the horse that has listened to every heart break and life changing event that has ever happened to me. I then look to Maddox, seeing the obvious sign of hope in his eyes. It's what softens the anger and the frustration I've been holding. He's trying. Trying to do what, I'm not sure. Repair a friendship?

Taking a deep breath, I slowly retreat. "I'll be back."

The breath of relief that expels from his mouth is visible when I spin on my heels and leave the barn.

Chapter Twenty-Seven

Maddox

Sugarfoot is saddled and ready when I hear footsteps coming up behind me. Clyde limps inside, a cigar dangling from his mouth.

"It's barely past noon, Clyde." I chuckle.

"Well son, when you hit seventy years old, you can do whatever the hell you want to," he grumbles.

He blows a puff of smoke before leaning up against Buster's stall. Cooper's horse. "You taking out Sugar?"

"Yeah. Me and Ivy," I say as I untie her from the gate.

"Ivy, huh?" He sucks on the stick of tobacco, his eyes squinting. "So, I guess you're finally doing something about that?"

I lift a brow. "About what?"

"You're a straight shooter, Maddox." He blows another puff of smoke. "I've seen how you look at her."

Clyde and his fucking observation skills.

"Yeah? Well maybe you should be working instead of watching me old man," I quip.

He laughs, deep and hoarse from years of smoking. "You're gone for her." He shakes his head, but his tone turns serious. "It's ok to do things for yourself sometimes, son. We both know your brother wasn't man enough to deserve her."

Hell, I don't deserve her either.

"But that boy never loved her." He keeps talking. "Not like you do."

I lead Sugarfoot down the alley way, walking past him in silence, not even sure how to respond.

He slaps a hand on my shoulder. "You deserve to be happy. Your pops would want that."

With a tight dip of my chin, I leave the barn. I spot Ivy walking down the porch steps, and I swear she just gets more beautiful every time I see her. When she approaches, she gives me a timid smile, her hands shoving into the back pockets of her jeans.

"You ready?" I ask.

She blows out a breath. "It's not like I have a choice, do I?"

"Put your boot in the stirrup." I've already repeated myself twice.

Ivy stands next to Sugarfoot, her hands clenched at her sides.

"I can't." Her voice is strained and her eyes pinched. "I'm not ready, Maddox."

"You *are* ready." I step over to her, running my hand up her back. "Now reach up and grab that saddle horn."

"I ca.." she starts, but I slide up farther to grip the nape of her neck. "That's the last time you say I can't."

I apply just enough pressure that her lip's part and I smile when her eyes flutter closed. We've been out here for two hours as she reacquaints herself with Sugarfoot. She's walked her and loped her in a circle. Pretty much everything that works up to this. To her facing her fear and putting that shit to rest. She loved it too much to never experience it again.

Something I can relate to.

"Now." I release her neck. "Get your ass on this horse."

She glares, her eyes shooting daggers at me as she dramatically slaps a hand on the saddle horn. "Happy?" She mutters.

"Not yet. Not until you're sitting pretty, darlin." I tap the seat of the saddle.

Gripping the horn, she concentrates on a deep breath, closing her eyes as she lets it out. Her left boot lifts to land in the stirrup, and she pauses when it's securely in place. "I'm scared."

I edge closer. Not close enough to interfere but close enough for her to feel safe.

"I know. But I'm right here. I won't let you get hurt."

"Gee, where have I heard that before?" She mocks. "You said that before, right? Or maybe I'm just confused," she scoffs.

"Ivy," I deadpan.

"Get back, Maddox." She grits her teeth.

With a tug from her arms and a swing of her leg, she catapults up to straddle the saddle, her body settling over Sugarfoot's back.

She's stiff, her thighs squeezing, showing off her discomfort. Sugarfoot shifts, so I place one hand on the bridle and one on Ivy's thigh.

"Woah," I say, stilling her movements.

Ivy tenses beneath my hand and I smooth my palm up her thigh. "Relax. She can feel how tense you are."

She closes her eyes, hands gripping the saddle horn as she mutters something under her breath.

"Good girl." I let loose of the bridle, letting my hand drift over Sugarfoot's neck while my eyes remain on Ivy.

Her eyes pop open and I can see her throat bob as she swallows at my words.

"We're gonna go slow, ok?" I squeeze her leg.

She nods. "Just give me a sec."

I let her take a few deep breaths before I gather the reins in my hand and step back.

"Ok." She relaxes her shoulders. "I'm ready."

I nod, and wade toward the pasture. "Wait," she calls. "Where's your horse? I thought we were riding."

I can see the slight panic in her eyes at the thought of me leaving.

"We are." I motion. "I'll be right here."

She frowns. "You're going to lead me? on foot?"

"Yes, Goldie. Today is about building trust remember?"

Her pink tongue slides out to wet her lips as she blinks. "Ok."

I smooch Sugarfoot along, following the path to the pasture that is free of ashes. The one that holds her flowers.

"Tell me about Georgia," I say, opening the gate.

"It's good," she says as the horse glides through the opening.

"Just good?" I shut the gate behind me, then continue my quest. "Come on. You liked it enough to stay for four years."

I glance back at her, and she clears her throat. "College was alright. I didn't do much but study and work. I waitressed at a local grill for the first couple of years."

"No partying?" I ask.

"You know I'm not the party girl type, Maddox," she deadpans.

I knew she wasn't, but I felt the need to confirm. To know she didn't leave here and completely leave behind the girl she was. *The girl I knew.*

"Boyfriends?" I ask the question cooly, but my insides are anything but.

"Some dates," she answers. "Nothing too serious."

Dates. Multiple. Why does that thought make me want to smash something?

We've made it across the pasture, just far enough to see the place I'm headed to in the distance.

"I work at a flower shop," she offers quietly.

"Yeah?" I glance over my shoulder.

"Yeah." A faint smile hits her lips. "I do the admin side. My friend Merit owns the shop. She handles the flowers, but I get to help and it..." she trails off.

"It what?" I ask, as I let go of the reins.

"It made me feel like I had a little bit of home with me."

Shoving my hands in my pockets, I continue walking as Sugarfoot follows. Ivy doesn't even realize I've let go. Her gaze is fixated across the miles of open acreage surrounding us.

"Did you ever miss..." I pause. *Me? Did you ever miss me?* I want to ask, but I don't. "Miss this," I finish.

I stop just at the edge of the field that leads to her favorite place. *The ridge.* When I look up to meet her eyes, they're glistening with moisture.

"I'm riding," she says quietly.

"You are." I keep my hands in my pockets and my feet planted.

A smile graces those perfect lips as she looks at me, then over at the ridge. "I did miss it." She faces me again. "I missed this."

Chapter Twenty-Eight

Ivy

A sharp knock at the door has me jolting. My clumsy hands spill the glass of tea I just poured onto the countertop. Snatching up a paper towel, I clean up the mess while simultaneously yelling, "come in!"

Dakota waltzes through the door, her hair curled and her *dance my ass* off jeans as she calls them covering her long legs.

"Don't give me that look." She shuts the door before propping her hands on her hips.

"Are you ok?" I ask.

I toss the towel in the trash as I scan her face. No signs of the heavy emotion I know that comes along with her father's sporadic phone calls.

"I'm great!" She hikes a thumb over her shoulder. "Shep here?"

Everyone around this town calls Maddox, Shep. Everyone but me.

"No, he was unsaddling Sugarfoot and had to check on the bulls." I realize my mistake when a perfect dark eyebrow lifts on her forehead.

"You went riding? With Maddox?" Her eyebrow stays intact, her arms crossing next.

"It wasn't a big deal." I wave her off.

It wasn't. I rode a horse for the first time in years. He walked next to me for over two hours. He took me to my favorite place. *Absolutely no big deal.*

"Ivy, that's huge." She smiles.

"It wasn't like we were riding off into the sunset." I walk around the bar and amble to the sofa. "He led me around. It was practically child's play."

"He led you?" She drops her arms and scurries around to fall down on the sofa next to me. "Where to?"

I hesitate, my cheeks heating. "The ridge."

Her grin spreads. "So, Maddox Sheppard spent the afternoon walking over a mile on foot just so you could get back on a horse for the first time?"

I roll my eyes. "Dakota."

"What?" She shrugs. "You want to tell me what that's about?"

No.

"It's not about anything." I pluck at a loose thread on the couch. "Coop suggested it. It's the only reason we went."

"Coop huh?" She levels me with her blue eyes. "It wasn't Coop taking you out to the ridge, was it?"

"Speaking of Cooper." I try to steer the conversation to safer territory.

Dakota is smart and can sniff out bullshit better than anyone I know. Which is why I've always avoided the subject of the cowboy in question.

"Ivy Mayson." She flicks my arm. "Stop changing the subject."

"There's nothing to tell." I throw my hands up, running them through my hair.

Her eyes soften just enough for me to realize; *she already knows.*

"How long have you known?" I ask while closing my eyes.

"A while." She crosses her legs. "I never really knew anything for certain. I just saw how he looked at you. How he's always looked at you when he thought no one was paying attention."

I sigh. "It's complicated. Was complicated," I correct.

She tilts her head. "Not anymore?"

"It's not a thing, Dakota. At one point in time there may have been some feelings, but it was just a phase. He was clear on that before I left. We are not.... there is not a *we.*" My stomach rolls at the notion.

"I disagree," she adds.

"It can't really work, Dakota," I scoff.

"And why not?"

"He's Brady's brother." I point out with a raised finger. "Laiken's brother." I point on another finger. "He works here at the ranch." I add another finger.

"All of those are facts, Ivy. Not reasons," she argues.

"Laiken would hate me," I voice. The other reason my guilt has always been so strong. "Who the hell dates both of her friend's brothers?"

"Ivy, you and Brady happened years ago. You were kids. You're an adult now. So is Maddox." Her hand reaches for me.

"I know that. But you know how this town is. You think we could just walk into the Mayson Jar hand in hand and live happily ever after?" I push to my feet. "No. There would be whispers, gossip, blame. Anything you can think of. I'd be labeled a *whore,* and whatever name they want to throw at me. Not to mention, Millie. She'd be heartbroken if I caused more rift between her children."

"Ok, I get it." She stands, placing her hands on my shoulders. "You got a lot going on right now. Which is why I came over."

I glance down at her jeans. "You have on your dancing jeans."

"I know." She waggles her brows. "We're going out. Cooper is rounding up the guys, and we are swinging by to grab Laiken."

"I don't really think I..." I begin but a slap to my ass has me yelping.

"Get moving." She points past me. "And wear your favorite dress with the yellow flowers."

I somehow find the will to allow my feet to move, but the thought of what happened the last time I wore that dress flashes in my mind.

But tonight, maybe I could forget.

Chapter Twenty-Nine

Ivy

The Mason Jar transforms from a quiet little café to a full-blown honky tonk once the clock strikes eight. The large room in the back is cleared of tables to make room for the dance floor, and the corner stage now houses a live band. As soon as we are inside, Dakota makes a beeline for the bar, while I follow Laiken to the other side of the room to snag a table. Cooper, Maddox, and Clyde are already sitting at a bar top table with a pitcher of beer and a couple of barflies lingering behind them. I recognize one from high school. Seems she never grew out of the *desperation* stage. Laiken hops up on the seat next to her brother, while I sit by Cooper, trying to avoid any accidental eye contact with the man across from me.

"Where's Ryder?" I ask as Cooper pours me a beer.

"He doesn't go out." He hands me the glass.

"What do you mean?" I frown.

"I mean, he rarely leaves the ranch unless it's for work purposes or to eat. He's practically a hermit."

A part of me feels for Ryder. I know he's still tore up over what happened eight years ago, but I figured he'd have at least moved on by now.

"That's sad." I sip my beer, scanning the crowd to see so many familiar faces.

When my eyes land on the bar, Dakota already has a tall cowboy leaning down into her space, a huge smile on his face. The poor sap will no doubt be buying her drinks tonight. She was an expert in harmless flirtation, and she did it well. Typically, it always ended up benefiting the whole group, so I had no objections to her antics. Except when I would catch the flash of hurt on Cooper's face. Like I just saw now. It's gone as quick as it came, and I watch Allison, one of the girls begging for anyone to give her a hint of attention, slip up next to him and whisper in his hear. She giggles as he stands, tugging her to the dance floor.

I glance at Laiken, who already has her phone out. "Laik. Trace is fine."

"I know." Her fingers move across her screen. "I'm just checking in. This is Hannah's first time babysitting."

Bless her mama heart. I hate that she feels guilty for having some time to herself. She deserves it more than anyone.

“Well look who decided to crawl out of his cabin?” I almost flinch at the sound of Brady’s voice behind me.

Maddox lifts his beer in salute, before knocking back a drink.

Does he normally not go out either?

I feel Brady’s hands land on my shoulders, squeezing lightly before he says. “Let me buy you a drink.”

I pick up my glass. “I've got one but thank you.”

“Ah, come on Ivy. It’s the least I can do.” He winks.

When he heads to the bar, I take a chance on flickering my eyes across the table. I should have known better, because as soon as I did, a slender arm wraps around Maddox’s neck, and my heart drops to the floor.

Two hours. Two whole hours I've had to endure watching Emily O'Connor flirt, dance, and practically grope Maddox on the dance floor. Memories from the night he shattered my heart into a million pieces plague my brain as I try to keep myself busy. I did everything in my power to avoid ending up in the crowd with Brady, but after the fourth time he asked for a dance, and when he didn't give me the opportunity to deny him, I let him lead me to the center of the floor.

"It's been a long time since we danced." He grins down at me, his hand sliding down to rest at my lower back.

"It has." I nod, swaying to the Zach Top song the band just started. "So, a fireman?" I ask.

He laughs, his eyes radiating pride before he speaks. "Yeah. I was in a bad way for a while there. Made a lot of mistakes." He swallows, meeting my eyes. "I wanted to do better."

I'm happy for him. Truly. I only ever wanted the best for Brady. We may not have been meant to be in a romantic aspect, but he was my friend. And I was rooting for him.

"I'm proud of you," I tell him. "It's an honorable job."

His hand slides up my back, the feeling leaving no tingles or any other reaction like it does when Maddox touches me. I immediately hate myself for the comparison.

"It's tough some days, but I feel like I'm finally on the right track. I've been trying harder with Maddox too," he admits.

They were working things out. Rebuilding their relationship. My heart squeezes at the thought, and my eyes involuntarily seek him out.

Peering over Brady's shoulder, I find Maddox across the dance floor, swaying similarly with Emily strapped to his chest.

It hurts.

Man, does it fucking hurt.

I thought four years was enough time. I was clearly wrong.

I wait for his searing gaze to turn back to her, but it doesn't lower to his dance partner. No, those hazel eyes remain pinned on me.

No words. We never really needed any. I could feel him with one look. His frustration. His *heat.* Tonight, it mirrored mine.

The song finally slows, and I pull away from Brady. "I'll be right back."

I maneuver past an older couple bickering, then squeeze by my brother who's dancing with Allison but clearly watching Dakota from across the room. His glare is unmistakable as her laugh reaches the dance floor. I'm almost free from the crowd when I feel a familiar set of hands slide over my hips.

"Dance with me, Goldie." Maddox's whisper sends chills racing down my spine, and I swallow as he pulls me into his hold.

My eyes scan for Emily as I turn, letting his palm splay across my back. Our hands join, and his thumb slowly glides back and forth along my skin as we begin to move to the new song.

"You remember the last time we danced?" He asks, his voice a whisper against my temple.

If I close my eyes I can see it clearly. The way the moonlight shined over the ridge. The way he held me. Just like this.

"Yeah." I clear my throat. "You taught me how to half step."

He changes our direction, spinning us to an area of the dance floor that's less populated.

"You seem upset."

I shake my head, my eyes still scanning the crowd. Like every single person here will see right through me if they look our way. Like they'll see my feelings are still controlled by this man who has no idea what he does to me. That he even still affects me.

"Not upset." I say, smiling at Penelope as she walks by. I offer a light tone. "You watching me, Shep?"

He frowns at the name. I've never called him Shep. "I know you," he murmurs, his lips brushing over my forehead. "For one, you never call me Shep," he says the words with a scoff.

"No, you don't know me." I bite back before he grips my hand, then uses his palm to push against my hip, spinning me out in front of him.

When he tugs, I'm surged back into his chest, his eyes casting down on me from underneath his hat.

"Bullshit." I gaze up at him as we stand frozen on the dance floor. The music is still playing, the dancers still in motion. Everyone is moving but us. "I know you. I know every fucking thing about you."

"Not anymore." I intended for the words to come out strong and confident, but it comes out weak and truth-less.

I can feel his hand slide from my lower back, up to the nape of my neck. His fingertips glide into my hair at the base, and he grips it lightly. With a slight readjustment, he tilts my head back, so I have nowhere to look but at his handsome face. It's taunting. Teasing, and I'm both angry and aroused as he peers down at me.

"I have one question" His voice his husky, his eyes hooded. He leans down, and I damn near moan when his lips brush the outside of my ear. "There a reason why you wore this dress tonight?" The hand that's in my hair loosens, and when the band cuts the song, he releases me.

My chest is heaving, my panties damp, and judging from the look in his eyes, he *knows.* Bastard. Instead of responding, I duck through the crowd and pray that he doesn't follow.

Slipping to the restroom, I lock myself in a stall and lower to the toilet. My hands go to my hair, my eyes closing as I reel in my breathing. This was one of the reasons I left. How could I spend the rest of my life watching him with someone else? Watching him get married. Have a family. Love someone else. Someone I can never be.

A lump forms in my throat, but I push it down. This only solidifies that as soon as we get everything handled with the ranch, I'll be back on the road to Georgia. Where I don't have to feel this shitty halo of circumstances hanging over my head all the time.

Stepping out of the stall, I quickly check my makeup before the door swings open and Emily steps in. She smiles, her long brown hair in waves and her jeans snug. She's pretty. Really pretty and it sends another stab to my heart.

"So." She grins. "Rumor has it there might be some rekindling with you and Brady?"

I snort a laugh, because despite how much I can't stand the thought of her with Maddox, she's never treated me dirty.

"Well, if you hear any of those rumors, you can squash them." I fluff my hair. "That ship sailed years ago."

"Too bad." She whips out her lip gloss. "I was hoping we could be sister-n-laws one day." She winks.

I feel the blood drain from my face, and without a word I spin on my boots and dart out of the bathroom.

I need to get out of here.

Now.

Chapter Thirty

Maddox

My eyes track Ivy as she maneuvers through the crowd and over to Dakota. I'm at the bar, waiting to pay my tab when she whispers something in Dakota's ear. Dakota nods, then digs out her keys, placing them in Ivy's hand.

She shouldn't be driving.

I don't think she's drunk, but it's excuse enough for me to follow her once she heads for the parking lot.

"Hey." Emily catches my arm before I'm past the end of the bar. "You mind taking me home tonight?" Her hand casually runs down the front of my shirt. "It's been a while." Her eyes blink with intention, but her persistent persuasion is getting old.

"Not tonight." I brush her off.

I can tell she's pissed at the rejection, but it's not like she's sitting at home waiting on me. She'll find someone else tonight, which is fine by me. A random hook up here or there when I would try to push Ivy out of my mind was all it ever was between us, and she's right. It's been a while. *Four fucking years.*

I should probably take her up on the offer, but instead, I'm again, casting my rational thoughts to the side and rushing out into the parking lot in search of Ivy.

I spot a wave of blonde hair as she trails through a row of trucks. My feet move, catching up to her quickly as I try to reach for the keys dangling from her fingertips. "You shouldn't be driving."

She lets out a screech, before slamming her hand to her chest. "What the hell, Maddox?"

"Give them here." I open my palm.

"No." She whirls around. "I'm fine."

Her tone is sharp, and I've known her long enough to know when she's pissed.

"Ivy," I grit out, gripping her by the crook of the elbow.

"Maddox, leave me alone." She rips her arm away. "Don't you have someone else to take home tonight?"

So that's what this is about?

"Are you fucking for real?" I scoff, stepping in front of her so she can't advance forward.

She turns back in the opposite direction, but I block that path as well, crowding her against a Dodge Ram.

"Let me go," she hisses.

My hands land on either side of her head, caging her against the vehicle. "You really think you have a right to feel hurt?"

"I don't know what you are even talking about," she snaps. "I don't want to be here, anymore. Please move."

I sear my gaze to hers. "Why?"

"It doesn't matter," she mutters, trying to duck out from under my arm.

I drop it, stopping her again.

"Why are you doing this? Just let me freaking leave!" She shrieks.

"Why? So, you don't have to watch me dance with her?" I tilt my head to the side, watching the way her eyes widen.

This is the first time we've talked about anything remotely close to these compressed feelings. The ones that have lingered between us for years.

"Stop it." Her chest rises, her breathing morphing into rapid pants.

"No, Ivy." I shake my head. "You don't get to run. You don't get to just take off when it hurts."

"I'm serious. Stop!" She shouts.

"You think it didn't hurt me?" I tap my chest with my fist. "You think it didn't rip me to fucking shreds to sit by for years while you fucked my brother?"

Hot anger fills her eyes, and she uses both palms to shove at my chest.

"You're an asshole." A sob catches in her throat as I stumble back into the car parked behind me.

She takes off, her brown flowered dress flying back behind her in her wake. *The same flowered dress from that night.*

"Ivy," I call.

"No!" She sobs. "Don't."

Regaining my balance, I lunge and catch her shoulders, turning her to face me. Tears stream down her face and regret slams into me. I use my thumb to swipe the tears from her cheeks, but she swats me away.

"I never slept with him."

I freeze. My hands dropping to my sides.

"What?" I ask in confusion.

She swipes at her tears again. "I never slept with your brother. Why do you think he was with every other girl that would spread her legs?"

Her confession has my pulse racing and my clumsy brain trying to catch up. "But.... four years?"

"Never." She shakes her head.

We stare at each other in the empty parking lot, the question burning on my tongue. For some reason I need to know. "Why?"

Her shoulder lifts in a light shrug.

So that means......fuck.

"Ivy." Her name tumbles from my mouth. It's painful.

"That night in the barn." Another tear trickles down her cheek. "I was a virgin."

I suck in a sharp breath, but before I can respond to the bomb that she just dropped on me, the door to the bar swings open, and a large body stumbles out, with Cooper's fist raised behind him.

Chapter Thirty-One

Ivy

"This is bullshit." Cooper scoffs next to me.

The fact he's riding bitch between me and Dakota in the back seat of Maddox's truck with a baby wipe shoved up his bleeding nose is comical.

"Well, I had it under control. I was three seconds away from inflicting permanent damage to his testicles." Dakota glares at him. "But you had to go and do some idiotic version of the flying squirrel across the whole damn bar."

"He grabbed your tits, Kota," Cooper growls.

Dakota glances down at her chest. "I mean, can you blame him?"

"I swear." He jerks out the wipe, shoving it inside his other nostril. "You need to be put on a leash from now on."

"A leash." She nudges his shoulder. "Who knew the golden retriever was kinky."

I bust out a laugh, Dakota joining me as he stares straight ahead. "I hate both of you right now."

"Cooper, she's right." Laiken glances back. "I've seen Dakota in action."

"That's right." Dakota winks.

"You should have seen her the last time Rhodes tried to get to Trace." Laiken laughs.

"When was this?" Maddox asks and Laiken stiffens immediately.

"Oh." She fidgets in her seat. "It was a long time ago."

Rhodes McDowell is Trace's so called father. *Biologically only*. He shows up randomly, pretending to give a shit. Trace doesn't even have his last name, but he tries to throw his weight around from time to time.

"Fuck, this hurts." Cooper whines, thankfully taking the heat off of Laiken.

"Poor baby." Dakota leans her head on his shoulder and slaps his thigh. "But thanks for defending my honor, Mayson. I'd punch a bitch for you too."

The cab grows silent, and I try to hang onto the lighter mood, but I catch Maddox's eyes in the rearview. Our conversation was interrupted, and I was kicking myself for letting my truths reveal themselves.

Why? Because he wasn't you?

Why? Because I held onto my virginity for you?

I could tell by the look on his face, he was in shock. Which means that conversation is far from over.

We drop Laiken off at Millie's. Twenty minutes later we're pulling up to the ranch. When we disperse from the vehicle, Dakota helps Cooper up the stairs to the loft, while I briskly walk down the path to Maddox's cabin. I want to crawl under the covers and hide. Pray he doesn't prod into anything further regarding his brother or what happed between us.

It's in the past. We've moved on.

Now you're lying to yourself, Ivy.

I make it to my room, shutting the door behind me as I lean back, sagging in relief. My head thuds against the wood as I wait to hear his footsteps. I'm filled with relief, but also a hint of disappointment when I hear him enter into his room and close the door.

I can't sleep. I've tossed and turned for hours, and the clock only reads three forty-seven in the morning when I glance at my phone. I groan, my hand gliding through my ratted hair before I drop it lazily back to the mattress. Climbing out of bed, I toss back the covers and creep across the room. I crack the door, listening for any sign of life before I tiptoe to the kitchen. As a kid, if I couldn't sleep, I'd wake up in the middle of the night, grab a spoon and eat ice cream straight from the container. Somehow, dad always knew when I was up, and he would join me. It didn't matter what time of night.

With my strawberry pint in my hand, I gently open the drawer to grab a spoon. When the first bite of sweet bliss hits my tongue, I close my eyes. But they fly open when I hear that raspy voice from behind me.

"Why?"

Chapter Thirty-Two

Maddox

Four Years Ago

I sit on the edge of the bed, disgust and guilt running its way through my veins. Emily scowls as she emerges from my bathroom.

"I got to shower." I push to my feet. "You can see yourself out."

I spent the entire fucking day watching Ivy at the trail ride. The entire day remembering what she felt like when I held her in my arms. I spent the entire day trying not to torture myself over something I can never have, when Emily appeared. It was a vast decision. One I hoped would rid my mind of everything Ivy Mayson. But that wasn't the case. It wasn't the case when Emily's mouth was on mine. It wasn't Emily's hair I fisted trying to chase a feeling that wasn't coming. It wasn't Emily's face I pictured when a hand landed over my jeans on my half limp dick. No, I saw golden hair and pouty plush lips with eyes so emerald you get lost. I couldn't do it, because she wasn't my Ivy.

I slam my bathroom door then take a quick shower, hoping Emily read the room and got the fuck out. I was an asshole for even making her part of my scheme. She didn't deserve that, and I knew it. Scrubbing a hand down my face, I wrap the towel around my waist and step back out into the living room when I spot Emily standing at my open door in nothing but my fucking t-shirt. Before I can ask why she thinks she has a right to wear my clothes, she edges open the door further, revealing a tear stained Ivy standing in the frame.

My gut sinks.

"If you're looking for Brady he's not here." Emily says as she twirls a piece of her hair between her fingers.

"Oh, I wasn't." Ivy's eyes meet mine, and the pain is damn near tangible.

She's upset and here I am half naked...with Emily in my shirt.

Motherfucker.

"Sorry to interrupt." Ivy turns while I quickly snatch up my jeans and shove my legs into them, before padding to the door barefoot.

"Where are you going?" Emily crosses her arms.

"Checking on Ivy. Make sure my brother is ok." It's a lie, but it rolls off my lips so smooth. "Take that off. We're done here." I say as I brush past her and down the stairs.

I hear her mutter something along the lines of "dickhead", but I ignore it, rushing to catch Ivy as she enters the barn. My long strides catch up to her, and I latch onto her elbow when she's made it past the second stall.

"Hey. You alright?"

Her brows furrow as she spins around and yanks out of my grip.

"Is it Brady?" I ask, knowing damn well it's not.

Her scoff is soft, and she blinks up at the ceiling. "No. God, not everything has to do with Brady!" Her voice is raised and her chest heaving. "Did you sleep with her?"

I palm the back of my neck, knowing I shouldn't let her think we did. My instinct is to push her away. To create distance. But the look on her face has me telling the truth. "No. I didn't sleep with her."

She rolls her lips together, her arms wrapping around her waist like she doesn't believe me.

"Were they just lies?" She asks, her voice cracking. "All those things you said?" Her eyes are not the ones I see in my dreams. They look haunted right now.

They're hurting and I hate it.

"What things?" My heart pounds.

"I won't let anyone ever hurt you again. I've wanted to hold you like this for so long. I can't breathe when you walk into the room. Am I a bad guy for wanting you? When you didn't belong to me?"

My entire body stiffens as she repeats my words. My confessions I thought were just whispered into a dark room. Fuck, I thought she was asleep. I would have never said those things out loud. For her to know them makes it real. And real means complicated. It means hurting him.

"You were drunk, Ivy."

She shakes her head. "I know what you said......"

"Why would I say those things? Especially to you?" I grind out.

I can see the physical flinch on her face at my words and it pisses me off. The fact I have to be the one to hurt her.

But she steels her expression. "You're lying."

I can feel the dirt beneath my bare feet. Feel the light breeze from the fan blowing above one of the stalls. Everything feels intensified.

"Look me in the eye and tell me you didn't mean it. Tell me you don't feel this, Maddox."

My chest pounds as she steps toward me. "Ivy," I warn.

Please don't come any closer.

"You can't say it, can you?" Her voice grows louder as she steps right up to me, her hands landing on my chest.

"Ivy...this is reckless." I wrap my fingers around her dainty wrists.

"I know," she whispers.

Her big green eyes peer up at me, and the thin cord that's kept me at bay for all these years, finally snaps.

Ivy

"Maddox." His name is on my lips, begging him to do something.

Anything. Tell me there's nothing between us. Tell me to leave. Take me to bed. Make me forget all the turmoil that this place holds.

Two strides. That's all it takes before his hands are in my hair, his lips on mine. It's not gentle. It's not sweet. It's frantic, it's sharp, it's full of need. Want. And raw hunger for each other. My hands dive into his dark strands, tugging as he lifts me from the ground with ease. My legs wrap around his narrow waist just as he moves, taking us through the open door of the tack room. My back slams into the wall and he groans when I nip at his bottom lip before sucking, before I run my tongue over it to ease the sting.

"Fuck," he rasps as he rips is mouth away, inching his lips across my jaw.

I shift my hips, causing his hard cock to settle right between my legs. The delicious friction solicitates a moan, and I circle my hips against him.

"Goldie," he growls, sucking hard on my neck before he slides one hand down to grip my ass. "Please tell me to stop. Tell me we can't do this."

I ignore his plea, my mind spinning as I feel his fingers slip inside the hem of my panties beneath my sundress. His callused fingertips travel over my drenched center.

"Soaked," he whispers in my ear before taking the sensitive lobe between his teeth.

"Maddox please." My back arches, my nails scrapping against his shoulders, with unhinged breaths.

I need him inside me like I need oxygen. I feel his hands leave me for only a brief moment, the sound of a zipper echoing inside the dim room before he reaches down to slide my panties back to the side. The smell of hay and leather surround us, but the hint of his cologne is what invades my senses. It overpowers me enough to have me not caring about the consequences of what's about to happen. The head of his bare cock presses against my entrance. His smooth skin warm and slick, and I grab at his shoulders to prepare for the intrusion.

"Words. Tell me you want this." His tongue swirls along my pulse point.

"I want this," I admit, my blood rushing at the adrenaline of this moment.

This inevitable moment. The moment I've been waiting for. To give myself to him. The moment is too tense for me to mention that small detail. That no man, not even his brother has ever been inside of me.

The second he enters me, my head rolls back, and I cry out his name as he thrusts deep, his forehead dropping to my shoulder. Pain shoots up my spine, and I dig my nails into his skin as he stretches me. His movements are hard, powerful, and my back drives into the wall with every piston of his hips. What began as a dull sting, has now transformed into a building pleasure. Pure and real. I know by the curl of my toes and the way he swells inside of me that this won't last long. We've had years of foreplay, and now, it's coming to a head. Like a volcano that can no longer withstand the pressure of the heat beneath it.

His lips meet mine again, our hot skin melting together with every thrust.

"Eyes." The word is whispered against my lips, and I pry open my lids, meeting his deep hazel stare.

"See me." His nostrils flare. "See who's making you come," he says, his thrust deep and full.

I nod just as he rotates, causing enough friction to my clit to have me soaring. My vision blurs, my thighs clench, and my moans bounce off the old wooden beams as I let the euphoria sweep me up. Maddox thrusts again, before his entire body tenses and he roars my name with those eyes still locked on mine.

Our movements turn sluggish, our bodies spent, as he plants lazy kisses on my jaw, then down my neck.

I sigh, my heart rate slowing as he gently lowers me to my feet after slipping out of me with a tenderness completely different than moments ago. The evidence of what we did leaks down my thighs, and in the moment of clarity, fear grips my heart. Maddox steps back, a buzzing sound vibrating on the floor beneath our feet. I move my gaze to the lit up screen as I drop my dress back in place.

There it is. The name flashing across his phone pours a layer of reality over the room.

Brady.

Maddox quickly zips up his jeans before swiping the phone from the floor. Guilt and regret are plastered across his face, and I try my hardest to clamp down the tears. He stares at the name, then moves his eyes to me.

"Ivy..." He shakes his head. "Fuck. I'm sorry. That..."

I reach out, but he backs away.

"That was a mistake." He runs a hand over his face. The one wearing the mask of betrayal. "I can't do this. We can't do this."

With tears clogging my throat I watch Maddox's back as he leaves.

He leaves me standing alone in the barn. And he never looked back.

Chapter Thirty-Three

Maddox

"Why?"

The question that has been taking over my mind for the last few hours tumbles from my mouth.

Why didn't she ever sleep with him?

She spins around, her eyes dropping to my bare chest, then to the joggers I stepped into before I impulsively came in here. I knew she was up, and as many times as I told myself to just *let it go,* I couldn't. She's driving me fucking crazy. Everything about her. Especially now that I know she gave me her virginity. In a dingy as fuck barn.

"Why what?" She asks, her eyes moving back up to mine.

"You know exactly what I'm talking about, Goldie." I round the table, stalking toward her.

She places her spoon and ice cream down on the counter. "Maddox, I..."

"It's a simple question." I reach her, my hands landing on the countertop next to her.

Her eyes cast down.

"Ivy, look at me." I lower my voice. "Not at the floor. Behind me, or at my chest." I lean in, waiting for her eyes to lock with mine. When she lifts them, they're swimming with tears. "Look right at me," I whisper. "And tell me why you never slept with him?"

She sucks in a sharp breath, and I can see the second she contemplates lying, but something flashes in her expression, and she narrows those emerald orbs. "You want the truth, Maddox?"

"Yes." *I've waited a long time for the truth.*

She's not touching me, but I can feel the heat from her skin. The tension between us so close to snapping. *Again.* She raises up on her toes before slightly adjusting her posture forward. Her soft lips meet the shell of my ear when she whispers the words that are my complete undoing.

"He wasn't you."

The control I've kept locked down for four long years is officially obliterated right in front of my eyes. My hands move to cup her face, my lips crashing to hers with an urgency I've never felt. I've never needed anyone like this. She gasps against me when my tongue licks along the seem of her lips, silently asking her to open. To let me see if she's tastes as sweet as I remember. Cause, fuck do I remember.

I've never been able to forget. She groans, her lips parting, her tongue battling with mine. I press myself against her tight body while her nails scrape at my skin. She tastes like strawberries and temptation. She tastes like what I've been missing for way too long. My hands leave her face, and drift down to grip her ample ass when I'm jolted back by her palms.

I blink my eyes as she brings her fingers to her lips, her head shaking.

"No," she croaks. "I can't."

"Ivy..." My hands itch to touch her, but she bolts across the kitchen. "You hurt me, Maddox."

My throat constricts. My lungs burning because she's right. I did hurt her.

I reach for her, but she flinches back. I swallow thickly, my words lodged as I prepare to tell her my truth, "I lied."

She slows her backward steps, her arms wrapping around her waist. "What do you mean?"

"That night." I run a hand through my hair. "When you showed up at the cabin. The last time...."

She bites her lip with a frown, her face pivoting to look out the window.

Shame fills me at the pain she's held onto.

"I lied about those things I said."

She whips her head around.

"The night you stayed with me. Those things I said to you." I slowly move into her space.

I won't let anyone ever hurt you again.

I've wanted to hold you like this for so long.

I can't breathe when you walk into the room.

Am I a bad guy for wanting you? When you didn't belong to me?

"I meant every fucking word."

Her hands drop. "You made me out to be a fool." Her words are like a knife to the chest. "You said I was *drunk*." Her voice grows. "You made me think I made it all up!" She shouts; her eyes wild. "That you would never feel that way about me, then you fuck me right after just to say it was a mistake."

"I know." I admit. "Fuck, I know baby. I'm sorry I hurt you." I bring my hands up to the back of my head. "I was scared. I was scared that if you knew how I really felt, it would be real. If it was real, then.... It would hurt him. I had already hurt him enough."

He'd barely forgiven me for the accident.

It's not lost on me that I made her a promise to never let anyone hurt her again. Then there I was, the one inflicting her heartache.

"I was wrong. And you will never understand how much I regret it," I admit.

She turns on her heels, her steps quick as she successfully escapes whatever the fuck is happening between us. I watch her go, letting the feeling sink in that it may already be too late.

Chapter Thirty-Four

Maddox

Eight years ago

The bright lights of the ambulance flash against the dark backdrop of the night sky. I numbly step out of the ambulance, my clothes bloody, but it's not my own.

"Let's get him to the OR." The paramedic behind me shifts me to the side so they can wheel out my father, who's unconscious on the gurney.

"Maddox, I need you to go with Steven. He will get you checked out." The paramedic carefully touches my arm, but I jerk away. "I'm fine. I'm going with him."

"He's in one of the best hospitals in the area. We got him." He motions to a nurse for a wheelchair as we enter the sliding glass doors. "Take him."

I watch the double doors at the end of the hall close behind the group of medical professionals that huddled around him the second we walked in. The ER may be quiet tonight, but inside, my world is chaos. My heart is racing, my brain foggy, and my boots soaked in a crimson stain.

"Sir. Would you like to call someone?" A woman with black rimmed glasses asks as she holds a clipboard to her chest.

Mindlessly, I walk away from the nurse who's supposed to be giving me my check over, and pull out my phone. The screen is cracked from the impact of my right leg against the door frame when we rolled along the asphalt.

I drop down into a cushioned chair, my head resting on my bloody palm as I dial my mother's number. She answers on the second ring, and I choke out the words that I already know will change our lives forever.

"Mom. There's been an accident."

My knee bounces, my gaze holding firm on the piece of shiny linoleum beneath my feet. Mom sits to my right, her arm looped around mine as she silently cries. Laiken sits on the other, her hands clasped tightly together as we wait for the surgeon to come out with the news that will determine if I will be fatherless or not.

"I'm so sorry." Pain sears through my chest when I say the words.

Mom grips my forearm with a quiet sob as she mindlessly caresses my arm.

All I remember is dad's booming voice. His frustrated words as I tried to tell him to slow down.

"Mrs. Sheppard?" The man in a pair of blue scrubs removes the mask from his face, his eyes regretful of what he's about to deliver.

"I'm Millie Sheppard." My mom stands, wiping the tears from her eyes. "How is he?" Laiken and I both push to our feet, her hand gripping mine as we wait.

"I'm so sorry," he says. "We did everything we could. The damage to his brain was too intense. We couldn't stop the bleeding."

The sob that breaks from my mother has my heart splitting straight down the middle. Laiken's knees almost buckle, but I catch her just as the sliding glass doors open. Brady rushes in, his boots leaving a trail of mud behind him as he sprints across the waiting room.

"What happened?" He gasps.

Mom faces him, her voice raw. "He's gone." She clutches her chest. "Your father is gone."

Brady's expression morphs into denial. "No." He looks to me. "What happened? You were supposed to pick him up!"

My throat closes up. "I did."

Tears pool in his eyes as he steps up to me. "You did?" He shouts. "Then where the fuck is he, Maddox?" He shouts.

The surgeon raises his hands. "Sir, I'm sorry for your loss." He addresses Brady. "The initial impact was severe. The oxygen to his brain was cut off almost automatically. He didn't suffer."

Brady brings his hands up to rest on the back of his head. Tears raining down his angry face. Dad was his idol. His person. The only one of us who really understood him. Brady had always been the kid who required the most attention, and dad had a way of handling him like we never could.

"He didn't suffer?" He scoffs. "He's fucking dead!" He bellows.

Mom's cries grow louder as Laiken wraps her arms around her, trying to soak up her pain.

The surgeon glances at me, a question in his eyes. The one I was dreading he would ask. "Was your father driving?"

A painful breath wedges within my lungs as I contemplate my answer. But when the doors open and an officer strides in, I do what dad would have done. I protect my family.

"No. I was."

The next thing I see is Brady's fist, along with the unforgettable words that I killed our father.

Chapter Thirty-Five

Ivy

I squint at the papers lying on top of this stupid piece of plywood. Acting as if I stare long enough, some magical plan will appear before me. I've been holed up in here all day. Avoiding the cabin and the man that has my nerves in a giant bundle. I snuck out of the house around five. I know from Maddox's routine that he usually leaves at six and I wanted to avoid him for a mile long list of reasons. My door had been closed, and I haven't come up for air once. I know Maddox has been across the hall for the last two hours. It's not like being locked up in here is helping. I've had that *kiss* on replay all day. The way my heart raced. My toes curled. It felt so automatic. Natural. And *terrifying.*

I barely get the papers gathered together when my phone rings. My mother's name is flashing across the screen.

"Hey mom," I answer.

"Hey sweetheart. We got a good update." I can hear the relief in her voice. "Your father's oxygen levels are good, so the doctor said we could possibly bust out of here tomorrow afternoon."

I lean back in my chair. "I bet dad's chomping at the bit."

She chuckles. "You have no idea. I just want to make sure you were still dropping off dinner. He's talked nonstop about Penelope's peach cobbler all day."

"Yes. I will be there." I pinch the bridge of my nose.

I had totally forgotten. I've spent more time obsessing over the reasons I can't forgive Maddox rather than handling my family.

"I'll be there around seven." I push to my feet.

"Perfect. Oh, and have her throw me in a piece of key lime pie."

"Yes ma'am." I hang up, and quickly dial The Mason Jar, rambling off my order to Fern.

Thankfully she's doesn't stay on the line to chat, so I gather my purse and my keys before heading for the door. I swing it open, my feet planting firmly when I come face to face with Maddox. His hazel eyes drink me in. Like he hasn't seen me in years, not hours.

"Hey." His voice has a rasp to it, and he clears his throat.

"Hey." I shut the door behind me then go to walk past him.

"Where you going?" He asks.

"The Mason Jar," I throw out over my shoulder. "I'm picking up food for mom and dad."

"Perfect."

I'm not sure why he says that, but I keep my feet moving forward to the safety of my car. When I reach the driver side door, I freeze.

"What are you doing?"

He opens the passenger side door. "Catching a ride. I happen to have a pickup order waiting on me."

My nostrils flare. "Maddox."

"It's a ride, Goldie." His head tilts to the side. "Don't overthink it."

I can feel my cheeks flush and I don't think it's from anger. I yank open my door, and slide in my seat as he closes his, folding his massive frame inside of my Chevy Trax.

"You okay over there?" I ask as he leans his head to the side. "You can scoot back."

He reaches beneath the seat, sliding it back all the way to fit his longs legs. "All set."

I nod, cranking the ignition and shifting into drive, trying to ignore the complication next to me.

Chapter Thirty-Six

Maddox

Ivy is stiff as a pair of starched jeans the entire drive to The Mayson Jar. We both pick up our orders and then continue to the hospital in silence. She's brewing. Processing and I understand what my lie did to her. On top of that, the barn sex, along with the way we just about devoured each other in my kitchen has both of us trying to sort out the situation. I'm still trying to figure out how something so fucking perfect can be wrong. How me wanting her and her wanting me is not in the cards. I'd never felt anything like I felt when I touched her. Nothing compares. But just because I told her the truth, doesn't make it any easier.

I was hoping it would at least help her understand what I feel. *For her.* That I've tried so hard to keep myself in check but her being here is killing me. Slowly breaking me down, and I'm not sure how much longer I can hold on.

I flicker my eyes over to Ivy. Her hair is piled on top of her head in some sort of elaborate bun. A few stray stands frame her sun kissed face and it makes me want to rip out my own heart. The one that hasn't stopped beating for her in four fucking years.

"I'll just be a minute," she says as we park.

"I think I'll come along."

What had me opting to go inside again to the one place I've avoided is something I'll never understand.

I push open the door as she mutters. "Of course you will."

I stride behind her, sure to keep my eyes peeled around the parking lot. I don't like her walking in this lot alone and I've told her that multiple times over the last few days. It's not quite dark yet, but it's getting there. I follow her quietly up to the third floor and out of the elevator. I'm checking a text from a stock contractor I work with regularly when I almost plow into Ivy's back. She's frozen halfway across the waiting room, the white sack of food dangling dangerously from her fingertips. My eyes move to where she's staring, then back to her.

"Why are you here?" Ivy's voice is strained, an undertone of aggravation resting beneath it.

"Ivy." Jamie, Aiden's wife stands, her eyes bouncing between us. "Aiden wanted to come visit Emmett."

I notice the way Ivy's breathing has increased. Her cheeks are a rose red, and her hands begin to tremble.

"You need to leave." Ivy lifts her chin.

Jamie rolls her lips, her eyes veering to the hallway. "Aiden will be back any minute and we wi...."

"I said leave!" Ivy grits out, her whole body beginning to shake.

What the fuck is going on?

"Ok." Jamie reaches down to pick up her purse, her eyes growing wet as she faces Ivy. "I'm so sorry, Ivy."

She scurries off as Ivy keeps her vacant gaze on her empty seat. I let my hand land on the small of her back, which jolts her out of her funk.

"Here." She shoves the food at me. "Please drop these off for me. I'm going to the bathroom."

Before I can ask what just transpired, she's down the hall and around the corner. Meanwhile, I'm left reeling with a bag of chicken fried steaks and a million questions.

Chapter Thirty-Seven

Ivy

My eyes are closed. My heart rate one single beat away from bursting through my chest as I suck in deep breaths. I don't know why I didn't prepare myself for this. The possibility of running into her. I pull my knees to my chest, my forehead resting on my kneecaps.

How fucking dare she come here.

The lump in my throat is beginning to hurt, and that initial anger that is resurfacing is brutal. A light tap on my stall door is vaguely heard through my ragged breathing.

"Ivy. It's me."

Maddox's deep soothing voice comes from beyond the other side.

"Can you unlock the door?" He asks.

I don't want to. I want to stay in this sterile box and hide. Not face any of my fears, but that's not reality, is it? Reality is messy. Unpredictable. Unfair.

That familiar need to let him be the one to wash away my problems blossoms inside of my chest. I lower my legs, rising to my feet before I flick the door lock. I can feel a fat tear drop drip down my cheek when I ease back the door. Maddox has his hands planted against the outside of the metal stall and his face draws up in a small scowl at my tears. Like he hates to see them.

"What do you need?" He asks, his voice low.

No interrogation. No questions about what happened. About why I spoke to Jamie that way. No. He only wants to know what *I* need. Which is why my stupid heart will never be able to let go of Maddox Sheppard.

"Home." I step into the open space between us. "I need you to take me home"

With a quick kiss to my forehead, he takes my hand, leads me down to the elevator, then to my car, where he places me in the passenger seat. He then maneuvers his body behind the wheel and drives me back to the cabin. His fingers never untwined from mine the entire way home.

I progress to the couch with a headache from the silent tears I let fall on the drive. I really just want to put on my sweats and curl up on the couch.

"Go change." Maddox motions to the bedroom.

Did he just read my mind?

He places his to go bag on the counter, pulling out two containers.

"I had already ordered for you before I knew you were going to the hospital."

And he got me dinner?

Here come the tears again.

"Peach Cobbler too," he adds.

That's it. I'm marrying him.

"Thanks." I turn away and escape to my room, where I pull on my old sweats and a ratty Reba McEntire t-shirt.

When I make it back into the kitchen, Maddox has both places set at the table. A cup is resting beside the container. A sweet tea, no ice, half full. Did Brady ever once remember that peach cobbler is my favorite or that I hate ice in my tea?

A small smile somehow crosses my face, even though my heart feels like it's been punched to death by a heavy weight champ.

Taking my seat, I watch him drop his lean body into the chair across from me. He doesn't begin to eat; he just folds his arms and studies me.

"Aren't you going to ask me?" I reach for my tea and take a sip.

He shrugs a shoulder. "I assume you'll talk when you're ready."

I nod and place the cup back on the table. "I think I'm ready." I meet his eyes, about to reveal something I've never told a living soul. A burden that isn't even mine to carry, but I do anyway. "Right before I left." I swallow hard, my mouth going dry before I rush out. "I found out my father and Jamie were having an affair."

Chapter Thirty-Eight

Ivy

Four years ago

"Sweetheart, we're out of cups." My mother moves to the large pot of chili before flinging her rag over her shoulder. "Can you run up to the house? I keep some plastic ones in the pantry on the top shelf."

It's our annual trial ride on the ranch, which consists of half of the town and those from the surrounding areas that come for a full day of riding, a chili cook off, live music, and family fun. Every year the crowd grows, and more people flock from all over to get a taste of the Mayson Ranch.

I glance at the toddler next to her feet, the smiling little boy is trying to steal a piece of bread from the table.

"Wylie." My mother playfully scolds. "Are you being sneaky?"

The two-year-old squeals when my mother dips to pick him up just as Aiden comes around the corner. "Sorry Ruthie. I was in a serious corn hole game. Jamie ran to the restroom, and I was on duty."

"Oh, this sweet boy ain't hurting anything." She plants a kiss on his cheek before passing him off to Aiden. Aiden and Jamie moved here a little over a year ago from New Mexico and I think Ryder and Cooper were finally glad to have another ranch hand closer to their age.

"Be right back." I call as I maneuver through the crowd, casually glancing around for the surly cowboy that had me twisted up for the last year. Maddox.

Instead of walking through the house, I take the pathway around to the back, planning to snatch the cups and get back as quickly as possible. I know how overwhelmed mom gets during this event. She doesn't want to let anyone down. I hop up to the screen porch, my hand wrapping around the metal latch when I hear my father's voice.

"You know this can't continue." It's stern, but not harsh.

"I know...I just..." The female voice is familiar, and I pause. "I've felt so alone, Emmett. And you were so..."

"It doesn't matter, Jamie." My dad's exhausted voice muffles through the screen.

My stomach begins to turn, a bad feeling rolling through me as my spine stiffens at her next words. "I know we are both married...."

No.

My stomach drops, my skin breaking out in a cold sweat. No, dad. Please no.

"If things were different," she continues.

My fingers hesitantly open the door, the screen making no sound as I peek through the crack and see my father standing in front of a tear faced Jamie.

Her greedy hands reach up and grip his old pearl snap shirt, and the worst thing I've ever seen in my entire life happens before my eyes. She presses a kiss to my father's lips. When he doesn't immediately shove her away, I step back, not realizing the sob that breaks from my chest. Both of their head's turn to mine, panic flashing across my father's face when he sees me retreat.

"Ivy!" He calls.

I turn to run, fresh tears falling down my cheeks at his blatant betrayal. The slam of the screen door sounds behind me.

"Ivy's please!" I feel his hand catch my wrist before he tugs me around to face him. "I'm so sorry." He brings me to his chest, and I want to curl up in his warmth and beat him with my fists at the same time.

I can't speak. I just push with my forearms before his hands cup my face. "I'm sorry." Tears fill his own eyes, and I see Jamie approach from behind him.

Backing away I glare at them both. Both of them broke the most sacred vows to people they claim to love. My parents took Aiden and Jamie under their wing. Took in their little boy like he was their own. And this is what they do. The pain this would bring my mother almost makes me double over.

"It was a mistake. It's over, Ivy. I swear to you." My dad runs a hand frantically through his hair.

"She's half your age." My words are groggy. "How could you?"

"Don't hate him, Ivy." Jamie begs. "It's not all his fault."

"How long?" I ask, as anger begins to settle in place of the initial shock.

"A month." My dad says before he puts space between him and Jamie.

"He's right. It was a mistake." Jamie wrings her hands together nervously. "Please, Ivy."

"I need to speak to my father. Alone." I straighten my shoulders.

With a quick nod, she swipes at the tears on her face and scurries off. I stare at my father, the man I've put up on a pedestal my entire life.

"Do you not love mom anymore?" I ask.

His eyes widen and his head shakes. "God, Ivy. No, I love your mother. So much. I made a mistake. I messed up, and I can't lose her. I can't lose...." His voice cracks.

His pleading seems sincere, but the evidence of his betrayal is too fresh. Too real.

"But you broke your vows." I clench my fists.

"I know," he admits with a pained voice.

"Are you going to tell her?" I press.

At the question his face pales. "Ivy. It would destroy her."

Then why? Why would he do this? Midlife crisis? Buy a fucking motorcycle like everyone else.

I've never hated him so much in my life. "This isn't just my life, Ivy. Jamie and Aiden have a son. He works for me."

So, multiple lives will be ruined for their mistakes. Their carelessness. Their lack of self-control.

"What are you asking me to do, dad?" I can hear the tremble in my voice.

"I'm asking you to not break your mother's heart."

That isn't fair. None of this is fair.

I let his words sink in before I respond. "You're right. It would break her heart, and I don't have the strength to do it." I turn to walk away, before peering at him over my shoulder. "But you didn't just break her's, dad. You just broke mine too."

I never got the cups. I ran straight to the one man who always put me back together. Only this time. He didn't.

Chapter Thirty-Nine

Ivy

"Jamie?" Maddox's eyebrows raise. "Aiden's Jamie?"

"Yeah." I nod. "I don't want to go into details. But I walked up on something I wasn't supposed to see. They saw me. My dad was crying. She was too. They both swore to me it was over."

He takes off his cap, placing it on the table. "Fuck, Ivy."

"He said it went on for a month. That they ended it, and he asked me not to tell my mother because it would break her heart. That it also involved Aiden and Wylie, and it would only make the situation worse on everyone." Even saying the words cause the memories to flood back. The ones I tried so hard to forget.

"I saw her kiss him," I whisper. "I hated him."

He leans forward, capturing my hand in his. "When did this happen?"

"The trail ride. The same night I came and...well. Emily was there and..." I trial off, not feeling like reliving that conversation again either.

Recognition appears in his eyes, and he closes them before cursing under his breath. "That's why you came to me?" I nod, while his thumb caresses my knuckles. "And I fucking pushed you away."

"It was for the best." I pull my hand away.

"The best?" He scoffs before he forces himself back from the table to stand. "How was what I did to you for the best, Ivy?"

"It turned out alright. I went to Georgia. Graduated college." I stand from my chair to match his stance.

"But you left!" His voice raises. "You left because of me?"

"No. I didn't."

"Don't lie to me." He's around the table now, his fingers lifting my chin to look into his eyes.

I count the seconds, preparing to admit yet another one of my truths. "I left because I couldn't look my mother in the eyes without guilt crushing my chest. I couldn't look at my father without resent clouding my brain, and I couldn't see Aiden walking on this ranch every day not having a clue what his wife did to him. I couldn't look at Jamie because every time I did, I wanted to strangle her." I take a deep breath just as his hand slides around to grip the nape of my neck. "And when I saw Emily with you." His forehead leans down to mine.

"I couldn't bear the thought of staying here to watch you fall in love with her." My voice cracks. "I know that doesn't sound fair. I was with Brady for years. But you didn't feel the same way about me. So, I ran."

Taking another deep breath, I roll my shoulders back. "I know that makes me a coward, but it's how I dealt with it."

"You're not the one who's a coward, Ivy." His jaw clenches and I'm not sure if he's referring to himself or my dad right now.

I take my seat again, and he takes his. "Can we just eat now? That was a lot to unload."

With a simple nod he grabs his fork, and we spend the next fifteen minutes in silence, while I process the fact that I just told my father's secret.

After we finished, Maddox left the kitchen. I don't blame him considering the grenade I just launched on a random Saturday. I know he cared for my dad, respected him, and Aiden is his friend. I trash the food boxes and wipe down the table before I head to the hallway with a plan to curl up in my bed and rewatch episodes of Heartland. When I pass Maddox's room, the door is ajar, and I glance through the opening as I walk by. Something catches my eyes that's lying on his nightstand. I press my palm to the door, tiptoeing in before I confirm that I hear the shower running behind the bathroom door across the hall. My bare feet carry me across his bedroom. His scent wrapping around me the farther I explore. When I get right up to the small wooden table, I peer down at the picture. Its half burned, but through the dirt and the ash I can see a smiling face. *Mine.* I pick it up, recognizing the picture my mother had framed in our old living room. I press my palm to my heart. He must have gotten it from the ruble. He found my picture. *And kept it.*

My legs are moving before my mind can catch up. My hand tentatively hovers over the doorknob to the bathroom before I throw out my insecurities and yank it open. My eyes land on a very wet and very naked Maddox. He's facing away from me, and even through the trickles of water filling the clear glass, I can see the vigorous muscles of his back. My heavy eyes trace over the curve of his firm ass, and down his thick legs. My core pulses and I grip the picture tighter in my hand. *Is he even real?*

My feet slide across the threshold, my heart nearly in my throat as I rip open the shower door next. Maddox doesn't even flinch. He uses both hands to run them through his hair after he dips his head beneath the spray. His wet ends curl and I completely stop breathing when he turns to face me, those hypnotizing eyes locking me in place. I drag my gaze down his chest, across his abdomen, then lower, where his steel cock twitches under my gaze. I've pictured Maddox Sheppard naked a thousand times. Even that night in the barn, our clothes didn't come off. But this. This version is beyond what my imagination could conjure.

"Goldie." The word is barely a whisper. Almost a plea as my eyes lock back on his.

Two beats. Two heartbeats, then he's reaching for my wrist and dragging me into the shower. Sweatpants and all.

Chapter Forty

Maddox

My arm bands around Ivy's waist before I crush her to my chest. The water cascades over her white t-shirt, melting into her perfect frame. Her gasp is audible inside the shower stall, and I quickly swallow it with my lips. I wasted precious time the first time I had her. She gave me something special, something delicate, and I did a shit job of handling it. I was rough, and impatient. A man driven by his emotions. Tonight, I was changing the game. I spent a long time on the sidelines. I watched my girl get heartbroken. I watched her bounce back. I watched her thrive in every area of life, while silently rooting for her from my corner. But I can no longer sit on the sidelines. I can no longer pretend that what this is, isn't real. It's the realest fucking thing I've ever felt. And right now, I plan to show her.

"Lift," I mutter the words against her lips, and she obeys without hesitation.

Her arms raise, and I use all of my ability to pull myself away long enough to peel her shirt from her body. The material slaps against tile floor where I deposit it, then my fingers slip into the waistband of her sweatpants. Falling down to my knees, I slowly trail the wet garment down her thighs, and to the floor. Her hands rest on my shoulders, using me as leverage as she gracefully steps out, standing beautiful and completely naked for me.

Leaning in, my tongue traces the path of a water droplet, leading down to the curve of her hip.

A soft moan sounds above me, followed by the feeling of her hands sliding into my hair.

"Maddox," she breathes out.

I press a kiss to her hip bone, before dragging my tongue across her stomach, then land another soft kiss on her other hip.

"I apologize, Ivy," I rasp out, looking up at her.

Her brows furrow, and her head slightly tilts in confusion. She's so fucking beautiful. Makeup free. Hair wet. Skin glistening.

"For what?" She asks.

"For our first time." I let my hands slide down to her thighs, kneading the smooth flesh beneath my fingertips. "You deserved better than some frantic fuck in a dusty old barn."

She smiles with a shake of her head. "I don't regret it, Maddox."

"I don't either." I hold her gaze. "But I do regret not treating you with the respect and attention you deserve."

Her hand runs through my hair, twirling one of the locks that I haven't cut in months.

"All that stops now," I declare. "From now on, when I have you, you'll be a withering mess before I'm through with you." One of my hands trial to the inside of her thigh, sliding up until I've reached the place I've dreamed about for years.

My fingers tease, my lips moving closer as she willingly parts those pretty thighs for me. She leans back, bracing herself against the shower wall.

Watching her expression, I lean in, blowing hot air against her swollen clit. Her eyes roll back, her hand clenching against my hair, giving me the confirmation that my girl likes the attention.

"Do you want to come, Goldie?" I ask, blowing just lightly enough that she raises her hips, begging for my mouth.

"Yes." She gasps. "Please."

Grinning, I reach up, removing the sprayer from the holder on the wall before I'm back in position. Lifting her leg, I place it over my shoulder. "I remember the way you looked." Two fingers slide over her slit, before I'm dipping them into her tight center. "The way your face flushed when you let go for me."

Her breathing hitches, her eyes widening when I pump my fingers. "I memorized it," I admit. "Because that was all I was going to get. I told myself I could never lose control again." I slide my hand out, and because I can't sit here any longer without a single taste, I let my tongue replace my fingers.

"Oh shi..." her thighs tense, and I grin against her wet skin.

She tastes like a dream, and regardless of how bad I want her to unravel on my tongue, I would rather see her face. Look into those daring green eyes as she falls apart for me.

I press a kiss to the inside of her knee, before I drop her foot back to the tile. She reaches for my shoulders, her nails scrapping against me in a silent plea for me to touch her.

"Spread your legs for me, baby." I twist the sprayer, angling it just the way I want it. "I want to watch you come."

Her pupils flare, and a sexy little vixen emerges right in front of me. A smirk tilts at her lips, her hands wandering down to her rosy nipples. She plucks them, as she inches her feet apart, creating the opening I need to make her forget she ever knew another man's name.

Lining up the head of the sprayer, I watch her lip's part when she feels the pressure against her clit. My free hand travels south again, wanting to feel the ways she squeezes me when she goes over the edge.

Her hands reach for my shoulders again, gripping and pinching as I work her with slow pumps and slight adjustments to the sprayer.

"Mad...." Her jaw drops slightly, her hips bucking to reach that moment of relief.

"That's it, Ivy baby," I coax, my lips landing on her neck as her head falls back against the shower wall. "Let go for me. Show me how good I make you come."

A strangled noise vibrates within my chest as I lean back, watching the most beautiful fucking sight I've ever seen on display right in front of me. Her body shakes while she cries my name, over and over.

Maddox. Maddox. Maddox.

My fucking name.

When her body is limp, and my cock achingly hard, I gently remove my hand and place the shower head back where it belongs. Her eyes are closed, and my heart thuds deep inside of my chest as I watch her lazily peel them open to look at me.

"Holy shit," she breathes out. "That was...."

I wrap her in my arms, never wanting to let this woman go. Her small palm winds between us, aiming to stroke my cock, but I grip her wrist, halting her pursuit. "Not tonight, Goldie."

She blinks. "But I..."

I press a kiss to her lips. "Tonight is about you," I murmur against her. "We got one on the books. Let's see how many more you can give me."

Chapter Forty-One

Ivy

Seven.

That's how many more I gave him last night and as I lay here staring at the ceiling, my body is feeling it. A blush breaks out over my skin when I glance over to Maddox, who's sleeping soundly on his stomach. His broad back is on full display, the sheet resting right at the curve of his ass. Which I know is covered in a pair of joggers because he refused to let me return any favors.

My heart warms at the thought. The fact he spent all night *making up* for the first time. But the unwelcome thoughts of how that night ended come hurling forward and a slight jolt of fear imbeds itself inside of my stomach. *What if he regrets it? Again?* Sliding the covers off of my legs, I swing them around in attempt to go to the bathroom and get something to eat when a hand catches my wrist. I peer over my shoulder, to see Maddox's sleepy eyes blink open.

"You sneaking out on me?" He asks, his voice husky from sleep.

"No." My answer is quick. A little too quick because he lifts a brow. I sigh, maneuvering around to bring my legs back up onto the bed. "No, I'm not sneaking out. I was just going to give you some space."

"Space." He says the word with distain. "I think we've had plenty of *space*, Ivy."

His fingers flex, and he drags me forward until I fall down next to him. His strong arm snakes around my waist before he's nuzzling my neck.

"Fucking space," he mutters under his breath.

Chuckling, I smooth my hand down his bare back, when a sudden pounding on the door has his head whipping up.

"Expecting anyone?" I ask.

"Not that I know of." He presses his palms into the mattress, lifting himself up.

"Shep! Open up!" The fist pounds again, followed by Cooper's voice.

Jumping into action, I bolt off the bed, my initial thoughts going to my dad. That something is wrong. Maddox follows, his feet thudding behind me as I jog to the door, unlock the deadbolt, and wretch it open. Cooper stands with his hands on his hips, his face serious. I can physically feel my soul fly out of my body when I notice the man standing right behind him.

Brady.

Cooper looks to Maddox before he's looking back at me. "We have a problem."

He brushes past me, and I motion my hand for Brady to enter. It's not like I could leave him standing on the porch. Which right now sounds better considering I was riding his brother's face at two this morning. When I close the door, Maddox is staring at me. He clears his throat, subtly gesturing a hand to my shirt. I glance down, my eyes widening. "Be right back."

I hadn't even realized I was wearing Maddox's t-shirt. I don't think Brady even noticed. He's already sitting down at the table. I make a quick exit, changing into some shorts and a tank top before brushing my teeth. When I'm back in the kitchen, all three have a cup of coffee in hand, patiently waiting on my attendance.

"Ok." I lean back against the counter. "What's going on?"

"Warren finished his report." Cooper shifts his eyes to Brady.

"And?" I press.

"He's ruling it an arson."

"What?" Maddox and I voice at the same time.

Cooper waves his hand in Brady's direction. "Tell them."

Brady braces his forearms on the table. "After my shift I hit the showers before I left. I was one of the last ones out, and when I was passing the chief's office, I heard him and Warren talking." He pauses, his hand scrubbing over his jaw. "He was telling chief about his findings. I heard the word arson and investigation."

"And you're sure it's about the ranch?" I question.

"Yeah. He said he was going to have to deliver the news to Emmett and Ruthie later today," Brady adds. "Look, I shouldn't be telling you any of this but if I was in your shoes, I'd want to know."

"Thank you, Brady." I reach forward and slightly squeeze his shoulder. "We appreciate it. Your name will not be mentioned."

He gives me a genuine smile, and I move my attention back to Cooper.

"Dad is supposed to go home today." I groan in frustration. "They don't even have a home." My head shakes as I hiss. "Apparently some asshole burned it down."

"They're going to stay with Penelope. I talked to mom this morning before Brady showed up." Cooper stands. "I want to be there when they give the news."

"Me too," I voice just as Maddox steps up next to me.

I can feel the subtle brush of his fingers against my back and it's shocking the sense of comfort it brings me. "Who the hell would burn down the ranch?"

Cooper levels me with a look. "Who do you think?"

"Oh, fuck," Maddox sighs.

Realization dawns on me. The only man who would benefit from our demise.

Rocky Bernard.

Chapter Forty-Two

Maddox

When the door closes, and Brady and Cooper are safely on the other side, I immediately wrap my arms around Ivy from behind. I hold her close, dropping a kiss into her hair before she spins in my arms.

"You ok?" I ask.

"I guess." She shrugs. "I'm not sure how I feel about that bastard burning down my home."

"I hate the guy as much as you do, but we have to be smart about this. You know he isn't sloppy if he even did this." I rub my hands over her shoulders. "Ryder is the one we need to worry about. His fuse has been short lately."

"Lately?" She scoffs. "He's been one spark away from detonating as long as I've known him."

I chuckle. “True.”

She presses a kiss to my cheek. “I’ve got some errands to run.” She smiles sweetly, and I know what that smile means.

She’s up to something.

“Ivy,” I warn.

“What?” She tiptoes around me.

“You’re not going over there,” I grit out.

“Where?” She picks up her pace as I follow her to her bedroom.

Her old bedroom. As of today.

“To Bernard’s.”

“And why do you think I would do that?” She snags up her favorite pair of boots, the ones she wore last night. I momentarily lose my train of thought as I picture them secured around my waist.

“Promise me,” I say, crossing my arms.

She pauses, her shoulders sagging. “I just want to talk to him.”

“And what? Ask him if he set your parent’s house on fire?” I ask, my voice growing.

Rocky is bad news, and I plan to keep her as far away from him as possible.

“I don’t know," she says as she shoves the other boot on her foot. “I’m kind of in a panic here.” She springs up from the bed. “If there’s an investigation this halts the insurance money. I’m not sure how much longer the ranch can hold out.”

“And you think confronting him is going to make a difference? We don’t even know if it was him.”

“Who else would it be?” She shouts. “Come on, Maddox.”

“Ok.” I raise my palms. “Baby, all I’m saying is *you* don’t need to be the one to approach him. Let me, Coop, and Ryder handle it.”

"Fine." She huffs. "But if I see him out in the wild, he's free game." She stands, pulling her hair up on top of her head, twisting it up into a bun. "I do need to get to the hospital. I need to help mom and dad get settled."

She steps up to me, her hands sliding around my waist. "What are you doing today?"

"What I do every day." I press a kiss to her forehead. "Why don't you take Dakota with you."

"I'll ask her. She usually doesn't have sessions on Sunday's."

Dakota is a horse trainer. A damn good one. She's even better than Cooper. I just don't want Ivy alone until we figure out what the hell is going on.

"Ok. I'm going to make my rounds." I lean back, watching the way her eyes hesitantly drift from mine. "Goldie."

"Mmhm," she responds.

"Do you want to talk about last night?" I ask, knowing her mind is reeling. Mine is too.

Brady showing up first thing this morning isn't helping either of us.

"Later?" She asks.

I nod. "Later."

The sun is already beginning to scorch the earth beneath it and it's barely nine in the morning. The air is still today, which is why I can clearly see the dust forming behind Laiken's SUV as she winds down the drive to the ranch. I had promised Trace he could come out once the fire had been cleaned up. She comes to a stop, and the back left door swings open. I can already hear her scolding him when his boots hit the dirt. Then he's in a full on sprint in my direction before she can even exit the vehicle.

"Trace Sheppard." She hisses. "You know the rules."

Dressed in his jeans, boots, and one of my hand me down cowboy hats from when I was a kid, the boy in question comes to a screeching stop when I cross my arms and lift a brow.

His big brown eyes widen when he sees my disappointment, and he hangs his head when my sister places a gentle hand on his shoulder.

"Sorry, mama," he says quietly before he looks up at her. "I just get excited about being a cowboy."

"I know that." She removes his hat and ruffles his copper-tinged hair before she drops a kiss there. "But you can't be a cowboy if you're in the hospital with a broken leg." She drops his hat back on his head with a quick look in my direction.

Laiken works at the local clinic, and in the summertime, instead of having to place Trace in daycare, he spends a lot of his days here with me. If I'm doing something where he can't tag along, he will spend time with Ruthie up at the big house or sometimes he even goes with Dakota. We all pitch in to help Laiken in whatever way we can. He hasn't been here in over a week, and I knew he was getting antsy.

"She's right buddy." I meet my sister's eyes, and she gives me a small smile.

His little brown boot kicks at the gravel before he sighs. "Yes ma'am."

"Alright. I'll pick you up this afternoon. I love you." Laiken turns to leave but Trace darts out, wrapping his slim arms around her waist.

"Love you more, mama."

Pride swells in my chest.

"Be careful." She narrows her eyes at me. "No bulls."

I lift my hands. "This is a ranch, Laik. I make no promises."

She shoots me a glare, but it's not heated.

With a pointed finger she backs up. "Take care of my baby. I don't want my deep cleaning day interrupted."

"Always do, sis," I counter before I reach down and grab Trace by the waist, flipping him upside down and over my shoulder.

He squeals in delight, his laughter making everything I work for worth it. Making this shitty week receive a little light.

"What are we doing today, Uncle Mads?" He asks.

I drop him to his feet and right his hat. "How do you feel about cleaning stalls?"

He shrivels his nose. "I gotta shovel shit?"

"Trace," I scold.

"What? I told mama you say foul words." He blinks up at me.

"Yeah. Because I'm a man."

"I'm a man too." He puffs out his chest. "Mama says I'm the man of the house."

Damn. There's that pinch. Pisses me off his dad didn't stick around to see what a good kid he is. He deserves better.

I crouch down. "How about this? You clean those stalls for me and after we can take a ride on Tater Tot."

He eyes the barn, then shoves his palm out to me for a firm handshake.

Just like a man.

"Deal."

Chapter Forty-Three

Ivy

"Where do you want this?" I hold up the basket full of socks and underwear that Mrs. Henson dropped off.

The one good thing about this town is if there's ever a tragedy, the forces are called in. I can't even count the number of casserole dishes that are scattered on my aunt's kitchen counter. Not to mention the bin of clothes that Millie wrangled up for my mom and Doc, our vet showed up with at least ten pairs of wranglers that are my father's size. I think it's just now hitting them what all was lost. Years worth of memories. But they had the necessities. Clothing, food, and toiletries. And a roof over their heads.

My father enters the living room, looking exactly the same as he did for most of my childhood. Wranglers, a plaid button-down shirt, and his snakeskin boots. His brown hair is now mixed with strands of gray, his walk a little slower, but he has the same warm eyes.

"You can just put it by the dining table," mom says. She points to the recliner. "Emmett. That's your spot for the next few days."

"Woman, I got cattle to check," he grumbles, before lifting the foil on a casserole dish to peek at the contents.

"The cattle can wait. That's what our sons are for," she fusses. "Your orders from the doctor are to rest."

"I'll rest when I'm dead." He winks at me, knowing he's just riling her up.

A flash of the past makes me smile. The way he used to tease her. Their easy banter that was so evident through my childhood. I think that was why his betrayal hit so hard. I never thought in a thousand years he would stray. He always doted on my mother and she on him. They *loved* each other. I knew it.

Even after his elaborate show of stubbornness, he shuffles to the chair and sits down.

"That's what I thought," she says, her eyebrows raised as she folds a pair of jeans.

Dad's smile is small, but I can still see the exhaustion in his eyes. The loss of so many things, and the unsettled situation between us. It's still nestled beneath the surface, and I know it needs to be addressed. After seeing Jamie last night, I was so angry. But I've had years to dissect the affair. The reasons. The consequences. I'm not sure if I'm hurting myself more than helping by reliving it all the time. Thinking of what I could have done different.

"Are you hungry?" I ask him.

"I could eat." He settles back. "Give me a variety."

Dakota has been manning the kitchen, so she hands me a plate, along with a serving spoon and I dish out a few scoops from different pans. I had just handed my father his plate when a knock came at the door.

"I'll grab it." My Aunt Penelope waves a hand.

I knew who it was. And deep down I knew this news wouldn't be taken well.

"Arson." My father's voice booms, and I flinch. "Someone burned down my house while I was in it?" His face hardens, his skin turning a shade of red that I haven't seen since I was a teenager.

"Emmett." My mom places her hands on his shoulders. "Let him talk."

Sam, the fire chief and my father's childhood friend sighs. "I know it's a shock. I assumed with the farmhouse being as old as it is, that it had some faulty wiring, or the furnace had issues." He runs a hand over his khakis.

"What did Warren find to make this conclusion?" My father asks, his eyes narrowed.

"The burn patterns. Warren concluded there was more than one point of origin." Sam exhales. "Did you see anything? Hear anything?"

"No. I was asleep in my chair in front of the tv. Ruthie was at book club." My father shakes his head. "I know exactly who did this."

"Emmett, we had to give this information to the police. They will take over the investigation. I need you to steer clear. Don't do anything stupid," he advises.

"You've known me my entire life, Sam. When have I been quick to strike?"

Sam chuckles. "Always. Which is why I need you to leave this to the professionals."

"Professionals," he scoffs. "Odis couldn't pour water out of a boot with the instructions on the heel."

Odis is the police chief, and has made quite the impression while in office. Considering he basically bought his position, my father isn't a fan, and of course, he's Rocky Bernard's younger brother so he automatically receives a negative reaction from my father.

"I don't disagree, but we have protocol." Sam's eyes drift over to my aunt who's standing next to my mom before he moves them back to my dad. "I'll keep you as updated as I can. It could take days, or weeks. I'm not sure. As of now, I would hold off on any insurance claims."

Dad nods, and my mom leans down to drop a comforting kiss on his head. "Thank you, Sam."

Sam pushes to his feet. "Of course." He glances at my aunt. "Penny."

She motions to the door. "I'll see you out."

Once she leaves, I meet Dakota's worried eyes from across the room before I face my dad. "What are we gonna do?"

His intense demeanor shows me exactly what we are going to do.

Get justice.

Chapter Forty-Four

Maddox

"Two Millers." I lift my hand as I call out the order to Shorty.

Brady finally dragged me out for *beers,* but it's hard to be relaxed when I haven't seen Ivy since this morning. The news, along with everything happening between us has my nerves shot to shit. We take the two barstools at the end of the bar at the Mayson Jar. It's quiet tonight. Sundays usually are and there's only a few other people mingling around.

"Here you go boys." Shorty drops the bottles down, before he's wiping down the rest of the bar.

"So, how's Ivy?" Brady asks before I even take my first drink.

"She's ok," I say before I take a gulp of the brew.

“I didn’t know she was staying with you,” he adds, and my instinct is to react with *what the fuck does it matter to you?*

But I just shrug. “With the big house gone, Coop didn’t have room. Her and Ryder are working on things so Cooper put her in Houston’s old room.”

He nods, taking his own drink. “I can’t believe someone did it intentionally.” He shakes his head. “That’s fucked up.”

“Yeah.” I use my thumb nail, peeling back the label as I try to figure out what to say.

We haven’t made small talk in years, and I never know how to navigate a conversation with him. In the past it always came back to dad, which then led to that night, which then led to yelling and punches thrown. So, I just wait for his que.

“Do you think Ivy would ever forgive me?” He asks.

The question startles me and gives me a feeling that has my chest tightening. "You’d have to ask her.”

He chuckles lightly. “I thought about it.” He takes a drink. “I know I fucked up. I know I wasn’t there for her.”

Yeah, I was.

“But she was there for me,” he continues. “When dad…” he trails off.

Dad and Ivy.

I would rather eat fresh cow shit than discuss either of these topics with him.

“I don’t know. I’m older now. Trying to get my life together. Ivy is the kind of woman that would make a good wife. She’d be loyal. Be a good mom."

I listen to him rattle off things about Ivy. Not a single one of those has to do with his feelings for her. It has to do with what she could be to him. Not once has he said that he missed her. Loved her. *Longed for her.*

"You think she'd give me another chance?" He questions next.

Considering she was climbing out of my bed this morning, probably not.

But I don't say that. I don't end the bullshit right now and tell him that I'm in love with her. *That she's mine.* I don't tell him not to ask her. Because at the end of the day, that's Ivy's choice.

"Don't know brother. Again. You'd have to ask her." I knock back a drink. "How's the station?" I ask, changing the topic to something not so fucking heavy.

"Good. I'm glad I did it. It sucks sometimes. Some calls are hard, but all in all I'm actually happy." He bumps his shoulder with mine. "How's your semen factory?"

A laugh barks from my chest. "Fuck off."

"Is that what you do all day? Jack off bulls?" He laughs.

Shaking my head I glance over at him and it's the first time I can remember that both of us are laughing. Together.

"It's an art really." I shrug.

"Damn." He finishes off his beer. "I'm glad you're doing something you love."

I nod, feeling that heavy weight again.

"I think dad would be proud," he says quietly.

"Yeah."

"Maddox." He pauses. "I'm..." he blows out a breath. "I've said some shitty things to you."

I slap a hand on his shoulder. "You don't have to say anything, Brady. I understand."

I can tell by the way his throat bobs he's getting choked up. I've made it my mission to help him move on. To help him get through the grief. Even when he was cursing my name. I took it. When he would get drunk, break things, and make my mom cry from worry. I knew he needed someone to blame. And instead of telling him the truth about our father. I let him blame me.

Chapter Forty-Five

Ivy

I stretch my arms over my head, my eyes growing blurry as I blink at the Excel sheet on my computer screen. Maddox was still gone when I got back to the cabin, so I decided to do some actual work. Merit had been so accommodating, and I couldn't let this cluster keep me from helping her. After all, it's only us two in the shop.

The lock clicks across the room, and I glance at the clock, seeing it's almost nine. Maddox enters, his hat coming off before he places it on the rack.

"Hey," I say, sitting my laptop on the coffee table.

"Hey," he responds as he walks across the room.

His eyes look tired, and he sighs deeply before stepping up behind me on the sofa. He leans down, pressing a kiss to the crown of my head, holding it there for a few beats too long, causing my heart to slowly start to enter into the realm of panic. I don't like how quiet he is, or how he walks silently over to the fridge and pulls out a bottle of water.

"Everything ok?" I ask, standing up on my bare feet.

It could be old feelings. Old worries slithering up my throat, causing the air in my lungs to falter.

He regrets it.

He gulps the whole bottle down before he finally meets my eyes. "We should talk."

Dread pools in my stomach and I swallow thickly. "Ok. About?"

"This." He motions between us.

I nod, leaning back to rest against the counter, all the way across the kitchen. Space is good. If he tells me that it was a mistake again, I won't have to smell his cologne.

He runs his thumb over his bottom lip before he speaks. "Have you forgiven him?"

I frown. "Forgiven who?"

"Brady."

I wasn't expecting that. Have I forgiven Brady? Yes. I did a long time ago. His actions don't hurt me anymore. Besides, what we have is an old friendship. It's childhood. It's not love.

"Yes. I have," I answer honestly.

He shoves both hands into the pockets of his jeans. "And if he asked you for another chance?"

"Where is this coming from?" I ask.

"We had drinks tonight." He shrugs. "He said some things."

I tilt my head to the side. "Maddox, Brady and I have been over for a long time. Even that last year, we both knew what it was. It wasn't love. It was comfort. It was honestly, on my end, obligation. I felt like I would be kicking him while he was down after your dad passed. I loved him. But almost in the way I love Cooper or Ryder." I push off the counter. "So, no. There will never be a second chance. Not for him."

I can see the quick flash of relief cross his eyes after he huffs out a breath. "Ivy, I understand if you want to see if there's anything left. I wouldn't stand in your way if that's what you really wanted. I want you to be happy."

Stepping right up to him, I place my finger over his parted lips. "Stop."

It's almost amusing to see the way his eyes bounce over my face. *He looks terrified.*

"There's nothing there. There can't be because my heart isn't available for him."

My hands reach out to land on his broad shoulders, and he removes his hands from his pockets.

"It's just...I know you two have a history." His eyes veer from mine, and it's the first time I've ever seen Maddox show any form of insecurity.

I push up on my toes, pressing a kiss on his stubbled jaw. "You have no idea how long I've been yours? Do you?"

Rough palms slide into my hair, and he tilts my head back. "Can you say that again, Goldie?"

"Which part?" I smile.

"The part where you say you're mine," he rasps.

"I'm yours," I repeat.

He drops his lips to mine in a soft kiss before he pulls away too soon.

"Can I be really honest with you here?" He asks.

I search those hazel depths and take a deep breath. "Yeah."

"I'm fucking petrified. Of this. Of how you make me feel." His hands shift, sliding down to my nape. "I've fought it for so long, and I'm just now in a place where me and my brother can have a conversation that doesn't end with him taking a swing. I'm scared this will be what destroys us. That he'll never forgive me." His forehead presses to mine. "I know you have a life in Georgia. I know you are only here temporarily. But despite all of those things..." He pulls back. "I can't stay away. Not anymore."

Cupping his jaw, tears fill my eyes. "I'm scared too. I would never want to be the thing that fractures your relationship with your family." He slips his hand down to link his fingers with mine. "But I've loved you since I was eighteen years old, and I don't know how to stop. I don't know how to make this feeling in my chest go away. I've tried," I admit. "God, did I try. I fled the state for God's sake." I laugh, but it comes out a sob. "I don't want to hurt anyone," I whisper. "But *I'm* tired of hurting."

His eyes are wide as he backs away from me and I watch his expression change from shock to maybe.... awe. I can physically feel the heat infiltrate my cheeks as I realize what I just did.

I just told Maddox that I *loved* him.

Shit.

"I'm sorry." I move to pull my hand from his.

God, what was I thinking? It's too soon. He's not ready. But he grips tighter, tugging me into his chest as his lips crash on mine. His kiss is deep, his heart pouring out with each movement. Soft lips melt to mine, and when he places a gentle peck on the corner of my mouth, he cranes his neck back to look down into my eyes.

"I love you too," he says.

Then he smiles.

Really smiles.

"Damn it, Ivy. I love you."

I can't help my own smile, but before I can say another word, he dips down, slinging me over his shoulder, and strides toward the bedroom.

Chapter Forty-Six

Maddox

Our shedded clothes cover my bedroom floor while Ivy's beautiful hair is fanned out over my pillow. Her big green eyes peer up at me as I climb up her naked body, my own eyes drinking in every delicate curve. Soft fingertips glide up my chest, and I drop my lips down to meet her collarbone. Legs parting, she opens herself up so I can settle between her hips, my leaking cock pressing against her hot skin.

A moan slips past her mouth when I lower, bringing her nipple between my teeth.

"Maddox. Please." Her breaths are choppy, and I lift my head to peer into her hooded eyes as I line myself up. Last time we did this, it was rushed. It was hard and fast. What we did was pure fucking. But tonight, I don't want to just *fuck* Ivy Mayson. I want to *love* her. *Make love* to her. Show her exactly how much I missed her. How long I've waited for her.

Her soft gasp at the pressure makes me twitch against her, and my hands grip the sheets as I steady myself. This woman has no idea that I haven't been able to be with anyone else. Not since her. Not since that night. I've been able to fly under the radar. Use work as an excuse for my busy days and lonely nights. But the truth is I didn't want anyone else. I only wanted *her.* And if it wasn't her. It was no one.

Slowly, I slide inside of her, our gazes locked, the world disappearing around us. It's always been that way when we were together. Everything else just fades away. She stretches around me, her legs wrapping around my waist with our foreheads coming together. My lips hover above hers as I seat myself fully inside of her. Her tight grip has me fighting back a curse. *I'm about to embarrass myself.* With a calculated movement, I pull out, just to thrust back in as deep as I can. Her throaty gasp fills the room, and when I feel her grin against my mouth, I press a kiss to her parted lips.

"I love you." The words are murmured against her, and I spent the rest of the night showing her just how much.

"Morning." Aiden walks into the barn just as I'm finishing up the white board.

"Morning." I snap the cap back on the dry erase marker and toss it in the bin.

The confession Ivy shared with me a few nights ago moves to the front of my mind, and part of me feels like shit for Aiden. Part of me feels like shit for Ruthie. And the other part is so damn disappointed in Emmett. But I know first-hand about hurting someone I love. Not in the same capacity, but still in the vicinity of self-sabotage.

"You see how Wizard is filling out?" He asks, adjusting his cowboy hat.

"I have." I grin. "Size wise he might beat out Havoc."

"Maybe." He shrugs. "He's already mean as shit." He grabs a pair of leather work gloves. "Catch you later."

He leaves the barn out the back exit, and as I'm turning back to the board, movement at the entrance has my eyes shifting. I'm surprised to see Emmett standing at the edge of the open barn.

"You supposed to be out here?" I ask.

He chuckles. "Shep, I've got three women up my ass right now telling me what to do. I don't need you to join in."

Laughing, we meet halfway through the alleyway, and I grip him in a hug. Emmett may have made some mistakes, but at the end of the day he was the only other father figure I've ever known. I wasn't happy about the position he put Ivy in, but it wasn't my place to bring it up. Not until they handled things between them, which I'm assuming hasn't been done yet.

Emmett pulls away, crossing his arms over his chest. "Cooper and Ryder will be here in a minute."

I can tell by the look in his eyes he has something on his mind. A few minutes later Cooper and Ryder show up, all of us aware of what's at stake.

Ryder shakes my hand, his eyes showing dark circles like he hadn't slept in days. Cooper slaps my shoulder before we circle up.

"What's on your mind, dad?" Ryder asks.

Emmett pulls a can of Copenhagen from his back pocket, taking a pinch between his fingers before stuffing it in his lip. "Rocky Bernard is trying to fuck with my ranch." He shoves the can back in his pocket. "He's been sniffing around for months. I'm almost certain that bacteria that took out half the herd last winter was him. Had no proof."

"We should have taken care of him when he was here," Ryder growls.

"When was he here?" Emmett asks.

"Morning after the fire. Showed up saying he wanted to check on his neighbors." Cooper scoffs. "Like he gives a shit. All he cares as about is money and he'll do anything to get it."

"We sent him packing." I shift on my boots. "Said some things to Ivy I didn't like."

Emmett practically vibrates with anger. "He's been trying to buy us out for years. My money is on him setting that fire, knowing we can't prove it. He did it so we can't get the insurance pay out. With all the back taxes on this place...."

"Shit," I mutter.

I had no idea it had gotten that bad.

"He's trying to force my hand," Emmett says.

"We all know Rocky doesn't do the dirty work," Ryder offers. "If he's behind it, he paid someone off."

"I agree," Cooper adds. "He's slick. He won't take a chance on tarnishing that fake ass reputation."

"What do you want us to do?" I ask. "Are we doing this off the record?"

"I'm not one to play dirty, but come after my family, *lawful* is off the table. We aren't playing fair anymore."

"We'll handle it." I look to Ryder.

"Let us feel it out." He tells his father.

"This time, I'll agree to step back. Your mother has me on a strict schedule. I had to get Sam to sneak me out here while her and Penelope went to the grocery store."

Cooper snickers. "And here I got my ass whipped with a twig for sneaking out."

Emmett gives him a pointed look. "Yeah, and look what good that did."

Laughs filter around before Emmett leaves the barn. We walk to the entrance, stepping out into the hot Texas sun.

"How do we want to play this boys?" Cooper asks.

I glance at Ryder who stares out at the empty pasture. "Something tells me he wouldn't chance physical evidence being found."

"So where do we start?" Cooper asks.

I know exactly where. The one who made the call.

Warren.

Chapter Forty-Seven

Ivy

I'm inside Sugarfoot's stall, running my fingers through her soft mane when I hear a throat clear. My father steps up to the stall, a smile on his face.

"You always loved horses. Ever since you were a baby." He reaches out across the gate to pet her neck. "Anytime your mama brought you out when we were working cattle you'd cry until she put you on the horse with me."

"I guess I never outgrew it." I shrug a shoulder.

"No. But you did grow up," he says, his eyes growing glassy.

I guess this is happening.

"Dad." I suck in a sharp breath.

He holds up a hand. "Let me get this out. It needs to be said."

I nod, continuing to keep my hands busy stroking Sugarfoot's back.

"I owe you an apology. I was wrong," he chokes out. "I was wrong to ask you not to tell your mother about me and Jamie. I was wrong for what I did. I was wrong for allowing my fear of the consequence to land on you."

I slow my movements, trying to breathe over the lump in my throat.

"I know I was one of the reasons you left. I know I played a part, and I'm sorry I made you feel like you couldn't be here. In your home. I broke your trust, and as a father, that's the ultimate failure."

Tears prick my eyes as I walk over to the gate.

He leans an elbow on the gate and meets my eyes. "Your mother knows. I told her about a year ago. I want you to know we did not get to the level of a sexual relationship."

"Dad. You don't have..." I begin.

"No, I do." He reaches out to grab my hand.

"We kissed. Three times. One of which you saw. The relationship was emotional more than anything, but that doesn't excuse my actions. It was inappropriate. My actions disrespected your mother, along with Aiden. It was a violation of my vows, and I take full responsibility. I love your mother with my whole heart. I was going through some things that I didn't handle well, and I let myself find comfort in the wrong place. Your mother knows that you know, and she holds no blame on you."

A sob rips from my chest as I yank open the gate and slide into my dad's arms. I let the tears fall. The ones that held all of my resentment, my anger, and my guilt.

He runs his hand over my hair. "I understand if you can't forgive me, Ivy. But just know that I love you."

"I love you too." I sniff.

In that moment, I knew I had forgiven him. I knew he held true regret, and the fact he told my mother, and owned his mistake speaks volumes.

"Mom said anything?" I ask, wiping my eyes.

"She won't. You know your mother. She's got the patience of a saint. She'll let you come to her when you're ready."

I pull away and look up at him, a small smile playing on my lips. "You know, I don't remember you having so much grey in your beard."

He chuckles and runs his finger over the mustache that he has repeatedly threatened to shave off. "I think it gives character."

"It sure does." I push up and press a kiss to his cheek. "I love you, dad."

We spent the next hour talking about Georgia. About my job at the flower shop. About Merit. About what all I missed when I was gone, including my mother's new addiction to historical romance. He was able to stay hidden in the barn with me until my mom and Penelope showed up and hauled him back to his recliner.

I had just given Sugarfoot a treat and was about to head inside to find Maddox and get supper started when I heard his voice raised outside of the barn.

"Laiken, slow down. What?" His voice carries panic, and I quicken my steps, darting out into the yard.

"Stay in the house and lock the door. I'm on my way." I watch him hang up, and the look on his face makes my stomach sink.

"What is it?"

"It's Laiken." He shoves his phone in his pocket. "I got to go."

When he moves toward his truck I follow. "I'm coming with you."

Chapter Forty-Eight

Maddox

I'm fuming by the time I pull into my mother's driveway. Rhodes is standing on the porch, his truck parked on the curb like he's been on a fucking month long bender.

Slamming on the breaks, I rip off my seatbelt before I face Ivy. "Stay in the truck."

I jump out, my rage boiling as the asshole yells at Laiken through the door.

"Rhodes." I call, taking long strides across the yard.

He turns at my voice, then saunters off the porch toward me. He looks like shit. His shirt is half unbuttoned, and his jeans wrinkled. He's been on the circuit, and clearly riding bulls has always been his priority. Not my sister. Or Trace. I've known him for the majority of my life, and quite frankly I've never liked him. He's arrogant, self centered, and a shitty father. I have no idea how someone like Laiken got caught up with him.

"Will you tell her I want to see my son," he bellows.

"I ain't telling her shit. You gave up that right when you decided you didn't have time for either of them. You aren't even listed on the birth certificate."

"This is bullshit," he barks. "I want to speak to Laiken. Now."

We meet up, toe to toe. "Best thing you can do is get off this property. You're trespassing."

"Fuck you, Maddox," he spits. "I got a right."

He moves quick, shoving me back a few steps. I react without another thought, throwing a solid punch that lands on his chin. He may be a prick, but he's tough. He falters only a second before he swings at me, clipping me on the temple, causing me to stumble backwards. When I lose my balance, I slam into a body, and I hear Ivy's painful cry behind my back.

Motherfucker.

Righting my feet, I whirl around to see her sliding down the front of the truck, clutching her back.

"Fuck!" I shout, crouching to grip her shoulders.

I ignore the chaos behind me, but I can faintly hear Laiken's voice before the wail of police sirens grow closer.

"Baby, look at me." I lift her chin. "Are you hurt?"

She shakes her head. "I'm ok. It just knocked the breath out of me." She winces.

Again, terrible liar.

I help her stand, feeling Laiken's hands land on my arm.

"Are you ok?" She squeezes my bicep before reaching for Ivy. "Oh my God, Ivy. I'm so sorry."

"I'm good." Ivy hugs her tight. "Are you ok? Where's Trace?"

"I'm good. He's inside." She looks to me. "I'm sorry. I didn't know who else to call."

"You always call me, Laik." I move to press a kiss to her hair.

When a squad car pulls into the drive, I notice Rhodes has already bailed. Jefferson, an officer we went to school with climbs out of the car and approaches.

"Maddox. Where is he?" He asks.

"He left." Laiken looks rattled. "He showed up, yelling and pounding on the door. He threatened to take Trace if I didn't let him see him. The same as always," she scoffs. "But he was off. He seemed like he was on something."

Jefferson glances at me. "You two get physical?"

"He made the first move," Ivy defends me. "Maddox was only protecting himself, Laiken, and Trace."

He nods. "Maybe he stayed close. I'll put a bolo out for his pickup. Still have the white Ford?"

"Yeah. He hasn't been by in almost a year. I wasn't prepared." Laiken shakes her head. "He just shows up sporadically."

"I'll let you know if we see him. In the meantime, he shows up again you call immediately."

"Thanks man, I appreciate it." I shake his hand before he walks back to his cruiser.

Hugging both girls to my chest I hear a small voice call from the porch.

"Mama? Is he gone?"

"Maddox. Seriously, I'm fine." Ivy is bent over the bathroom counter while I clean the cut across her back.

Fine my ass. She bled right through her damn shirt.

"I told you to stay in the truck," I grit out.

"Yeah, well I wasn't just going to sit there and let him hit you."

"And what were you going to do?" I swipe an alcohol wipe over the cut. "I don't want you around him anymore than I want Laiken around him."

"You forgot I know him too, Maddox." She rolls her eyes. "He's usually a bunch of talk."

He was. Rhodes had always been mouthy, and it always got him into trouble.

"Can you just do me a favor next time and listen to me?" I ask as I smooth a Toy Story band aide over the cut.

"We'll see," she sasses.

Lowering her shirt, I swat her ass before spinning her around. "Just agree."

"And what do I get for agreeing?" She muses, her eyes dropping to my lips.

I wrap an arm around her waist and press a kiss to her sexy smirk.

She opens for me just as a knock sounds behind the bathroom door. We jolt apart, before Laiken slips in.

"You ok, Ivy?" She asks in concern.

Ivy clears her throat. "Yeah. All good. Maddox patched me up."

I can see the nervousness in the way her hands fidget.

"Thanks," she says as she brushes past Laiken.

We've been in our bubble for the last few days. It's clear us being in the open may be a different story.

Chapter Forty-Nine

Ivy

My heart felt lighter after clearing the air with my dad, but I still felt a twinge of guilt after Laiken almost caught Maddox and me in the bathroom. The way my stomach pitted. It wasn't that I was embarrassed to be with Maddox, but I felt like if we were going to do this, it needed to start with us being honest. With each other. With Laiken. With Brady. The longer we keep this a secret, the more damage it will do. *I should know.*

I place the last curl in my hair, then spray some hairspray on the blonde strand. I hated that Dakota's birthday was in the middle of all of this, and I hated that it was also on a day that was hard for Maddox. It's the anniversary of his father's death, and even though it's been over ten years now, I know the grief doesn't ever go away.

I feel a pair of hands slide around my waist as I lean in to check my makeup.

"You look beautiful, darlin." Maddox says against my hair.

I smile. "Thanks. You don't look so bad yourself."

He's wearing a teal pearl snap that makes his eyes pop against his tan skin.

"You sure you want to go? I understand if you would rather have a quiet evening." I watch him through the mirror.

"No. The day doesn't get any easier. Sitting home alone and over-thinking isn't what dad would want. I'll have my moment with him when I need to."

I smile. "You're a good man, Maddox Sheppard."

He places a kiss on my neck. "Not good enough for you, Goldie."

Spinning around I watch him adjust his belt, clasping the buckle he won years ago.

"I talked to dad."

"Yeah? How'd it go?" He asks.

I roll my lips. "Good. He apologized, and we worked it out."

He reaches out to tug on one of my curls. "I'm happy for you. I know it's been wearing on you."

I reach for my lips gloss. "Yeah. I feel so much lighter already."

"Can I offer some advice?" He tips up my chin.

"Speak, oh wise one," I tease.

"I know it's hard to think of your dad as anything but this perfect man who does no wrong. As kids we idolize them. We think they don't make mistakes or make bad choices. But the best thing you can do is not let your love be conditioned by who he is to other people. To your mom. To your brothers." He places a kiss on my temple. "You love him for who he is to you."

I close my eyes. "Thank you."

He cups my jaw, then presses a kiss to my lips. "Anytime."

Warmth spreads at his beautiful words, but my nerves swarm as I prepare to say mine. "I think we should tell your family."

He pauses his exit from the bathroom.

"I mean, your sister. Brady. I want us to......" I close my eyes. "I don't want to hide my feelings for you anymore. I don't want to have to jump away from you if someone walks into a room."

His eyes blink, his face emotionless.

"Or not," I whisper. "If you don't want this to be exclusive, we don't have..."

"Goldie," he says, casually crowding my space, causing my ass to press into the counter behind me. "This is exclusive."

He towers over me, his hazel eyes a wonderful storm. "I want this. You and me."

I sigh in relief, and my forehead drops to his chest. "Thank God."

He chuckles. "I thought I made myself clear when I confessed my undying love."

I swat at his hip. "Shut up. A girl just needs a little confirmation before she potentially destroys a family."

He grips my face in his hands. "This is not on you, Ivy. This is two people who love each other. And if Brady loves us both, he'll understand."

I sure hope he's right.

Chapter Fifty

Ivy

The bar is calm tonight. It's the middle of the week, so after we ate dinner, we conjured around a table at the back and watched one of our hometown bands take the stage. Dakota is adorned in a white cowboy hat, complete with a tiara and a leopard sash that says *birthday bitch.* Cooper has drug her across the dance floor for half of the night, while the other half she's spent dancing with random old timers and a few teenage boys who are living their cowgirl dream.

Ryder of course didn't attend, and I was surprised Laiken showed after yesterday's event with Rhodes, but she looked like she could use a beer and some two stepping. I haven't danced with Maddox yet, and I wonder if that's even more noticeable than if we danced every song. I don't know how to navigate this with him. In the open. I know we agreed to tell his family, but tonight it's not happening. Tonight, we are still hidden behind closed doors. Still a secret. *Will I ever escape those?* Downing the last of my drink, I hop down from the stool.

"Be back boys," I tell Hoss and Waylon.

They salute me with their drinks as I weave through a few empty tables until I'm ducking into the bathroom. I handle business quickly, before checking myself in the mirror then head back out to the table. I get two steps down the hall when Maddox rounds the corner. He glances over his shoulder, I'm assuming to confirm the coast is clear, before he reaches for my face, gripping my jaw in his overpowering hands.

"I've been wanting to kiss you all fucking night," he admits as he slams his lips on mine.

I whimper when his tongue lashes out to taste me, the simple act causing my nipples to tingle in anticipation. He walks me back until we reach a door to what I'm assuming is some sort of supply closet. His hand drops behind me, twisting the knob before he nudges it open with the toe of his boot.

"Inside." The deep timber of his voice sends a jolt straight between my legs, and I slowly walk backwards as he stalks toward me. Shutting the door behind him, his eyes trail over me, his hand dropping to the bulge growing behind his zipper. I lick my lips, the urge to taste him hitting me like an unexpected tsunami.

"See something you want?" He taunts.

I nod, and he palms his jeans. "You want this, Goldie?"

"Yes." My answer is breathy, and I move my impatient hands to help him unclasp his buckle, then unbutton his jeans.

I drop to my knees before he can tell me otherwise. With eager hands, I pull out his hard length and stroke him from root to tip. His head falls back. His groan deep and brutal. Harboring my confidence, I let my tongue out to lick his pulsing tip, before I suck him into my mouth. A curse flies from his lips, before his hand is in my hair, guiding my movements along. My own hands grip his thighs as I take him deeper.

"Look at you, Ivy baby," he praises. "Sucking me so good."

I moan around him, and the vibration sets him off, a deep growl echoing in the small room before I'm yanked up from the floor. His mouth is on me, his hands bunching up my skirt as he guides me toward a bench in the corner. His tongue spears mine before he spins me around, then he drops down to the bench.

"Spread," he rasps.

I peer at him over my shoulder as he grips his cock, the tip leaking over onto his thumb when he strokes himself. I oblige, spreading my legs as my skirt pools around my waist. His fingertips reach down, sliding my panties to the side, allowing me the freedom to hover over his lap.

"Sit." The next order is combined with him pressing into my soaking center.

When he enters me, my head drops back, resting against his forehead as his magical fingers land on my clit. He strums a tortuous rhythm, his hips thrusting upward to dive into me with wild abandonment.

"So good," he murmurs. "Always so fucking good."

"So good," I repeat before a throaty moan expels from my body.

My core tightens, my blood rushing when he thrusts hard and bites down on my shoulder. One more tight circle of his thumb and I ignite. My release hits me full speed, the ultimate bliss flowing through my veins as I ride out my orgasm. He's still making long languid strokes, one hand wrapping around my waist to steady me. Just before my body sags, he stills, his hips jerking as he empties himself inside of me, the words *I love you,* groaned out with every drop.

When we finally catch our breath, he lands a few soothing kisses on my shoulder before he lifts me, depositing me back on the floor so I can fix my clothes.

I smooth down my top. "How do I look?"

He smirks. "Thoroughly fucked."

"Shut up." I roll my eyes. "We need to look normal."

He buckles his belt, then slides his hands along my jaw to tenderly hold my face. "I don't like hiding this."

"I know," I whisper before he drops a soft kiss on my lips. "You go out first."

He studies me for a moment before he nods, then leaves the room. I count to thirty, then slip out into the hallway, hoping no one is none the wiser.

We managed to make it out completely satisfied and unscathed, so I'm trying not to engage in too much activity or the undeniable evidence of what happened in that supply closet will be running down my legs. Sipping on my drink, I watch Laiken and Maddox glide across the saw dust floor. He spins her around just as I hear a ruckus from the front. Peeking over my shoulder, I spot Brady. He's barely walking in a straight line, while Emily is tucked up under his arm.

Great.

They stumble in, both appearing to be three sheets to the wind.

I glance to the dance floor, trying to catch eyes with Maddox. He meets mine, before drifting them to the doorway. I can see a small curse fly from his lips and Laiken follows his line of sight.

I'm sitting by Hoss, one of the younger ranch hands who lifts an arm to wave at Brady.

"Ivy Mayson." Brady slurs, as he and Emily approach the table. "Gorgeous as always."

Emily rolls her eyes before she unhooks his arm from around her shoulder.

"How about a dance, babe?" He leans in, his whiskey breath fanning over my face.

"You're drunk, Brady." I let out a light laugh, trying to keep the tension light. "Let's get you some water."

"I don't need water." He runs his hand over my hair. "I need a dance."

"Brady." Maddox's voice comes from behind him, his expression stern.

"Brother!" He lifts his hands in the air.

I can see the concern on Maddox's face. We all know what day it is, and over the years we've never been sure how Brady chooses to cope. Obviously, he chose alcohol this time.

"How about a shot?" Brady points to Maddox, before pointing at Cooper. "You in?"

My eyes track Emily as she slithers up next to Maddox and reaches up for his hat. She plucks it from his head, smiling as she goes to lower it onto hers. Before she can drop it in place, he snatches it from her hand and shoves it back on his head.

Everyone around here knows what that means.

His hat. His girl.

"Maddox." She pouts. "You know what it means for me to wear that!"

"I know exactly what it means." He hardens his jaw.

"So, you're saying I'm not your girl?" She questions.

Our eyes meet briefly before he glances at her again. "No, you're not." He tips his head in Brady's direction. "Didn't you come in here with him tonight?"

She grins, her smile calculating as she makes eye contact with me. "I was just trying out the Ivy method. Why stop at one brother when you can have both?"

Chapter Fifty-One

Maddox

I watch the color drain from Ivy's face, Emily's eyes twinkle in satisfaction.

"Emily," I grit out.

"What?" She shrugs.

"What is she talking about?" Brady chuckles and glances at Ivy.

"They didn't tell you?" Emily crosses her arms.

"Emily. Now isn't the time," I warn.

He frowns. "What is she talking about, Maddox?"

Fuck. Not tonight. Definitely not tonight.

"Nothing. Why don't I get you home."

"She's been fucking him," Emily sneers. "Has been for years."

Ivy jumps from the stool, her eyes frantic.

Brady looks at her, before looking at me. "Ivy? And you?" He lets out a dry laugh. "No way. She wouldn't even spread those pretty little legs for me."

"Watch your fucking mouth," I snap, taking one step farther to bump my chest with his.

Her searches my face, and he must see it, because he scoffs. "Wow." He looks over to Ivy. "So that's why you ended us. You were too busy riding my brother's dick?"

"Brady," Ivy hisses. "It wasn't like that. And how dare you when you were screwing anything with a pulse."

"It wasn't like that huh?" Emily waltzes up to Ivy. "What happened in the barn, Ivy?" She lifts a brow. "I followed y'all." She peers back at me. "I'm pretty sure what I saw was fucking." She faces Ivy, her hands planted on her hips. "I would know. He's fucked me plenty of times."

The hurt on Ivy's face practically rips my heart out. I bolt toward Emily, right when Brady's fist connects with my jaw. Shaking my head, I lunge, tackling him to the ground before he can do any more damage. Loud voices filter around me, and I feel two arms catapult me off of him. Cooper holds my arms, as Hoss and Shorty wrangle Brady.

"You stole her from me!" Brady yells as he fights against their hold. "You took him from me too," he spits. "You took dad, and you just couldn't help yourself. You had to take her too."

"Enough!" Shorty growls. "Penelope, call the station!"

"You good?" Cooper asks as I break from his grip.

"I'm fine," I grit out. My eyes scan for Ivy, and when I find her, Emily is still in her face, spewing her venom that I take complete responsibility for.

I take one stride on the way to my girl when Laiken comes out of nowhere, her palm meeting Emily's cheek with a force I had no idea she had in her.

"That's the last time you will insult her or my brothers." Laiken's tone is sharp, her eyes blazing.

Holy shit, I've never seen Laiken even get remotely angry.

"Don't worry guys. I'll take out the trash." Dakota saunters up, grabbing a fist full of Emily's hair before leading her out the exit, kicking and screaming.

I look around the room, examining the shit show that just took place when my gaze lands on Ivy in my sister's arms. And I'm terrified that I just lost her.

After the officers spoke with Penelope, I convinced them to let Laiken take Brady home. The last thing he needed was a night in jail to compromise his place at the fire house and I knew tonight was just a bad night in general. Add in the Emily show, and he was bound to blow.

Dakota has her arm around Ivy. I watch them leave through the front entrance as I walk over to Cooper.

"Ivy is driving Dakota," he says, running a hand over his clean shaved face.

"I'm sorry it came out this way." I palm my neck. "We planned to have a normal conversation and let everyone know."

Cooper just shakes his head. "I've known for a long time, Maddox. Honestly, I was surprised it hadn't happened yet."

"You knew?" I ask.

Amusement shines on his face. "You demanded to be the one to care for Ivy's horse when she left. In *my* barn." He points to his chest. "You staked your claim in a lot of subtle ways, man. And I caught on pretty quick."

"And what do you think about it?"

I shove my hands in the pockets of my jeans, waiting on his answer.

"I think if you make each other happy, what else matters?" He slaps my shoulder. "Let's go Romeo. I'll drive."

Chapter Fifty-Two

Ivy

"Here." Dakota hands me a t-shirt and I tug it on before climbing up into her loft bed in the trailer.

It's a tight fit, but I've slept on beds much smaller with her when we were kids. Sighing, I bring the handmade quilt up to my chest and stare at the ceiling.

"Is that JB Mauney?" I laugh.

"Hell, yeah it is." She climbs up next to me, pointing to the poster taped to the interior of the trailer over the bed. "Who needs a man when I have JB to keep me company at night." She winks.

Such a Dakota thing to say.

We both settle back, neither of us talking about the cluster that just unfolded. I felt like I had done enough damage tonight, which is why

I'm currently in this horse trailer instead of in the cabin with Maddox. He needs to think. Have a chance to process just like I do.

"I'm sorry I ruined your birthday," I say quietly.

She rolls her head to the side to look at me. "*You* didn't ruin anything, Ivy. And don't give that bitch so much credit."

My throat clogs, tears burning my eyes when I think of the things she said.

I would know. He's fucked me plenty of times.

The look of betrayal on Brady's face. The anger on Maddox's. All because of me.

"You and Maddox did nothing wrong," she assures me.

I nod silently, swiping at a stray tear.

"And don't worry about, Emily. She's found other things to occupy her time."

"Like?" I ask hesitantly.

"For one, growing in that bald spot I left on her head." She grins.

"Dakota." My scolding tone makes her giggle.

"She deserved it for hurting my family."

My heart swells in my chest. Dakota doesn't have a *family,* and I'm honored to be considered for the role.

"Thank you," I whisper.

"Always," she says back.

We grow silent, the exhaustion of the night taking over when my phone vibrates.

Maddox: No matter what. I love you.

More tears spill as I send a simple response.

Ivy: I love you too.

I wake up the next morning to a dead phone, and a loud fist pounding on the trailer door. I swear this has become the new norm for my alarm. Dakota groans, so I crawl down, shoving the door open as the sun assaults my eyes. It's Cooper, his brow furrowed and his face serious.

What now?

"I've been calling you since six."

"My phone died. What's wrong?"

"Mom called. She's been at the station all night. They brought dad in for questioning."

"What?" I blink. "Questioning?"

"About the fire. Apparently, they did it under the guise of just regular questioning, but it turned into an interrogation."

"Interrogation?" I frown. "They think he did it?"

Cooper tosses a hand up. "I don't know what they fucking think, but he didn't do it, Ivy."

"Ok." I pinch the bridge of my nose. "Let me get dressed and we can go get her."

He nods. "I've got the guys lined out. I'll be by the truck." He pauses and his eyes veer over my shoulder. "She hungover?"

"A little." I turn back to hear her snoring softly. "You know, her. She goes big or goes home."

"Ain't that the truth," he mutters before he motions for me to move. "You get dressed. I'll leave her out some Tylenol and water. If I don't, she'll forget."

I watch him step over her last night's clothes and I wonder when the day will come that Dakota will see what's right in front of her.

Chapter Fifty-Three

Maddox

The sunlight shines through the trees as I make my way across the Mayson Ridge cemetery. Dad's headstone is the last one on the eighth row. A large arched slab that reads his name, and below, his favorite bible verse is engraved in cursive font. My chest tightens the closer I get, the feeling of disappointment wracking my bones. What would dad think of what happened? Of my actions? Of Brady's?

Stopping in front of the stone covered with flowers I know my mother puts out every few weeks, I crouch down.

"Hey dad." I lower my head. "I fucked up pretty good."

Silence greets me, like all of our conversations and it stings.

"I tried so hard to stand in your place. To lead our family like you would have wanted me to." I feel my throat swell. "But I'm not you, dad. Mom is lonely. Laiken is worn out. She's trying so hard to be both parents. I did what I thought was the best way to help her. All she ever wanted was to go to school." I pick at a clump of loose dirt, letting it disintegrate between my fingers. "She thinks she got a scholarship for school." I clear my throat. "I knew she'd never allow me to pay for her classes, so I made up a scholarship and put a large chunk of my rodeo earnings in there to put her through college. Trace was just a baby, and she was struggling. I wanted her to beat the odds. For her to still achieve her dreams even as a single mother."

I small breeze blows through the aisle, and I reach up to touch his name.

Morris Sheppard.

"You were her biggest cheerleader. You'd be proud of her." I let my fingers drop. "And Brady. You two were so much alike. Wearing your heart on your sleeve." I shake my head. "He blames me. He believes I'm responsible for what happened." Letting my eyes fall closed, I speak the words that have held me captive for years. "And I let him. Because I love him too much to let him be hurt by the truth. To let him know that you made mistakes, just like everyone else."

I can feel the wet stains trailing down my cheeks. "It doesn't matter that you were the one driving that night. I should have stopped you. I should have made you give me those keys. I knew you had been drinking." Fuck, my chest burns. "I didn't want one mistake to define you. I didn't want Brady, and Laiken, and mom to think you were anything other than the man you always were to us. A good father. A good husband. Loyal."

My thighs burn as I push to stand. "You once told me to always put your family first. And right now, I am. Brady is my brother. I love him. But Ivy is my family too. I love her so much, dad. And it's fucking killing me that there isn't a world where I can have both."

Bending down I right one of the horse figurines that fell over. "I miss you. I wish you were here to tell me what to do. To tell me how to fix this."

When more silence engulfs me, I take one last look at the headstone and turn to leave. When my eyes raise, a few feet behind me stands my brother. I walk toward him, neither of us speaking as I pass him, heading to my truck that's parked just beyond the fence.

When I make it back to the ranch, Laiken's SUV is waiting by my office. Climbing out of my truck, I slip on my hat before she meets me around the hood.

"Hey." She reaches up and touches my chin. "He clocked you good, huh?"

I scoff out a version of a laugh as I rest against the grill of my truck. "I saw him at the cemetery this morning."

She nods. "Yeah, I figured."

"None of this is Ivy's fault," I say, my immediate reaction jumping to defend her.

Laiken smiles softly. "It's no one's fault, Maddox. You love who you love. Sometimes we don't get to choose."

"You saying that about Rhodes?" I lift a brow.

She snorts. "God, no. I never loved him."

It makes me wonder if she's ever loved anyone. The look in her eyes says she understands, but she's always been private.

"I came to tell you that Brady may be upset, but he'll get over it. He's a big boy. We can't always shield him from everything."

"I know that." I sigh. "We just wanted to do it the right way. Sit him down and tell him. Tell you and mom. Ivy is afraid y'all will resent her if it drives a wedge between us."

"I would never resent her. As far as Brady, don't let it drive a wedge. Talk to him. Tell him how you feel. Honesty might actually be what he needs, Maddox. Not protection."

She raises up and presses a kiss to my cheek. Her hot pink scrubs are like a beacon of light out in this colorless dirt. "I just wanted to check on you. I've gotta get back to work. I've got Mr. Norman today and he's ready to get back to his regular poker nights and out of his wheelchair."

Chuckling I walk over and open her car door. "Love you, Mads."

"Love you." I slam the door and head to the cabin.

I'm walking up the front steps when I spot it. Right there on the doormat. *A wildflower.*

Chapter Fifty-Four

Ivy

Three hours. I had been sitting at the police station with my mom and Cooper for three hours, waiting on my father to leave the interrogation room. Cooper finally had enough and got Jefferson to go back and check on him. My father's tired figure comes strolling down the hall with Chief Bernard behind him, a smug smile on his face. It was clear who's side he was on.

"We'll keep in touch," he says as my father storms toward us.

We scatter to our vehicles in silence until we arrive at Penelope's. As soon as we get into the room, my father picks up the first thing he sees and fires it against the wall, shattering the glass flower vase.

We sit stunned, as his chest heaves. "I should have known better than to voice my concern. To tell them who I think sabotaged my ranch."

We all know who he means, and the fact his brother was all smiles tells me he's absolutely right.

"What did they say, dad?" Cooper asks.

My father drops down into the recliner with defeat. "They asked questions about what I saw. Where I was. Who could have access to the property. Of course I told them Bernard has the most to gain, in which that was ignored." He shakes his head. "That's when the gaslighting started. When the *chief* stepped in. He brought up the taxes and somehow had inside information on the ranch. How deep we are in dept."

"Shit," Cooper hisses.

"They accused you?" I gasp. "For insurance fraud?"

"Basically. Stated I could have burned it for the insurance money, which I can't even claim because it's been ruled an arson."

"So long story short, they aren't going to do shit, and we can't file a claim." Cooper stands, pacing the living room. "Regardless of if you set the fire or not, since we didn't file a claim, there is no crime."

"I didn't burn down my home," my dad grits out. "And now, we're going to lose it."

"We won't lose it, dad. We'll figure it out." I tell him, reaching for his hand.

He drops his head back on the cushion of the recliner. "I'm not sure there's a way to come back from this." he admits quietly. "And I can't." He closes his eyes. "I can't sell it."

I glance over to see my mother's determined gaze.

"There's always a way," she states.

It was almost sundown by the time me and Cooper got back to the ranch. I was nervous, but something told me it was time to face Maddox. With every foot I planted on the front porch, the more nauseated I got. What if he wanted to end it? What if the damage was already done? With a deep breath I twist the handle, entering the quiet cabin. I freeze when I see Maddox sitting on the couch in the dim light. His forearms braced on his knees.

I close the door behind me, before walking slowly around the couch and over to him. I hesitate before he pats the spot next to him. I lower myself down, my eyes landing on a tin box he has perched on the coffee table.

"I missed you," he confesses, staring at the box.

I reach over, sliding my hand into his large one. "I missed you too."

Sitting by the box is the flower I had left for him this morning. It's an Indian Paintbrush.

"I missed you every day after you left," he says, his free hand moving toward the box. "Even though I was the one who pushed you away, I always kept a part of you with me."

He uses his callused fingers to flip open the lid to the box. My breath catches in my throat when he reveals the contents.

"You kept them?" My voice is barely above a whisper.

He lifts his head and meets my eyes. "Every single one."

Looking back down at the box, I take in the wilted petals and dried out stems. The once beautiful flowers are only twigs now, but they are stacked neatly with care. Some even keeping their shape.

He kept them all. *Every single wildflower.*

"Maddox. I won't ask you to choose me." I close my eyes, my heart aching and fluttering in tandem. "He's your brother."

"It's already a done deal, darlin." His smooth voice hits my ears. "Four years ago, I didn't choose you. And I don't plan on making that mistake again."

I feel his fingers on my chin, guiding my face to his. "I love you. I want to spend my days leading you around this ranch on Sugarfoot or whatever horse you choose. I want to bring you your favorite peach cobbler home on a bad day. I want to listen to your laugh, and if you want to pick every single flower in the state of Texas, we can do that too."

A tear slides from my eye, and he catches it with his thumb. "I'm all in. Me and you, baby."

Smiling, I lean in, pressing my lips to his. "I love you."

Pushing off of the couch, I crawl over to straddle his lap, my arms wrapping around his neck.

"Are you sure?" I ask, my teeth sinking into my bottom lip.

Smirking, he lifts the cowboy hat from his head, and places it gently on mine. A grin blooms between my cheeks.

"Maddox Sheppard. Are you saying what I think you're saying?"

His smile is devastating. "It's pretty simple, Goldie. My hat. My girl."

Chapter Fifty-Five

Maddox

I finally managed to pull myself away from Ivy's naked body in the shower to drag my ass to work. She had some computer stuff to do for the flower shop this morning, then she was going into town to have lunch with Laiken and Dakota before stopping by to see her parents.

I had just left the breeding barn after checking in on a sample when I spotted Ryder on horseback. He had been MIA since before the fiasco at the bar.

Waving him down, I walk along the fence line until he rides up next to me.

"Hey," he huffs out after dragging the bandana down he had tied around his mouth.

"You alright?" I ask.

"Fine." He shrugs. "Just making sure everything is settled."

He rests his hands on the saddle horn, and I don't miss his bloody and scrapped knuckles.

"Anything you want to share?" I prod.

He spits on the dirt. "Nope."

Knowing Ryder, he went rogue. Maybe even tried to handle business himself. We hadn't made a solid plan for confronting Bernard yet. I was just waiting on my instructions

"What did you do?" I motion to his bruised knuckles. "Get in a fight with a t-post?"

He chuckles and glances out over the bull pens behind me. "Looks like you got a shiner yourself."

I smirk, knowing my lip is still busted and my jaw is beginning to bruise. "Conversations with my brother."

He nods. "I heard." Doesn't surprise me. Nothing is kept secret for long in this town. "Way I see it, she picked you. End of story. Don't know why it's anyone else's business.

"Thanks." He may not have said the exact words, but he just gave me his blessing.

"I got to get back. Doc is coming out today to check the herd." He pulls up his bandana and rides off before I can toss anymore questions his way.

Something tells me Ryder has been busy. And it didn't have anything to do with cattle.

Two hours later I've got my two bulls that are needed for my next sample separated and the ones under contract for a rodeo about thirty miles south pinned on the back side of the barn. I walk around the building, shaking the dust from my jeans when Brady's truck pulls up the drive. I watch him park before he steps out and meets me in the middle of the gravel.

He motions to the office. "Got a sec?"

"Sure." I lead the way, stopping to grab two bottles of water from the fridge in the small kitchen inside of the office door.

Tossing him one, I walk past him and into my office, dropping back in my chair.

He sits in the seat across from me, his eyes trained on the water bottle in his hand.

"Why didn't you tell me about dad?" He asks. "That he was the one driving?"

I let my hands rest on the arms of the chair. "I don't know. I thought I was protecting you. Protecting his memory."

"You let me say some awful shit to you." He looks up. "You let me treat you like an outsider for something you didn't do."

"Brady..." I start.

"Did you do it because you felt guilty? About Ivy? That you deserved my hate because how you felt about her?"

No. Maybe?

"We wanted to tell you together. To explain what happened." I run a hand down my face.

"What Emily said about the barn? When was that?" He asks.

His tone isn't accusing, it's almost as if he's surprised that he missed the signs.

"It was almost a year after y'all broke up. I swear to you, Brady. Nothing ever happened while you two were together. Ivy was loyal, and I respected your relationship."

He nods, then looks up at me. "Did you love her? Even then?"

"Truth is I've been in love with her for a long time. Probably before I really even understood what it was or what it meant," I admit. "But you were..." I pause and consider my words. "My brother. Important to me and after the night in the barn, when things turned physical, I panicked. I pushed her away. I told her it was a mistake." I lean my elbows down on the desk. "I chose you, Brady."

His eyes widen before I continue. "I chose you because deep down I knew she was just as scared as I was. We both loved you, but we loved each other too."

He glances away, before facing me again.

"I chose you, Brady," I repeat. "But I can't choose you again. Not this time."

He searches my face for a second before he surprises me.

"I need to apologize." He stands. "For blaming you. For holding you accountable when it was an accident. For not taking responsibility for my fuck ups." He pounds his chest. "That's on me. I loved Ivy in my own way. She was one of my best friends. But I can be man enough to admit that I never was in love with her. Not the way you are. Not the way I see it in your eyes when you talk about her. I didn't think about her after she left. Maybe a random thought or two. Maybe when I saw something that reminded me of her. But I didn't *miss* her. Not like I should have."

I push to my feet and round the desk.

"What I'm trying to say is, I want you both to be happy. And I'm glad that it's with each other. You deserve to be happy, Maddox. So does she."

Lifting my arms I grip him in a hug, an embrace I haven't felt in a very long time.

"I should probably apologize to Ivy too about the things I said," he offers before stepping back.

I hear his words, but my gaze is locked over his shoulder as my Goldie stands in the doorway. Her beautiful smile wide.

"Here's your chance, brother."

Chapter Fifty-Six

Ivy

"Talk to me." Maddox places a kiss on my knee before he parts my legs and nestles his way between my thighs.

I laugh, placing my laptop on the coffee table before laying back against the arm of the couch.

After the talk with Brady, we spent the remainder of the day taking a walk out to the ridge on Sugarfoot, before we came back to cook us something to eat. Brady apologized for the things he said, for the things he did when we were together, and I've never seen him and Maddox be in a better place. Millie even called to congratulate us on our new relationship and told me she loved me. Another person I was sure would write me off. I've never been happier, but at the same time

I've never felt a deep sadness like the one I feel when I think about losing this place. Losing my *childhood.*

"I don't know what to do," I admit.

He presses a kiss to my neck. "You'll figure it out."

I turn my head, giving him full access as he continues to pepper soft kisses along my skin.

"Dad will never sell. He'll go down fighting." I close my eyes.

"Reminds me of someone else I know," he murmurs against me.

"I know this place is his pride and joy, but what if he did sell? He could come out with some money to put back. Buy him and mom a nice place. He won't have to be out of the house at sunup and coming in at sunset. He could retire."

Maddox leans up, resting his head on my stomach. "That sounds nice, Goldie. But being a rancher never ends. Not for men like your dad. Or his father, or the ones before him. This land is Mayson land. Always will be. He has dreams to pass this place down. See his grandchildren running through the pastures. This ranch is who your dad is, baby. It's in his blood. That's why he'll never sell. He wouldn't be just giving up his own dream, he'd be giving up his legacy."

I reach up, running a hand through his messy hair. "When did you get so smart?

"Probably around the time you were earning that business degree," he taunts.

"Please. You were living your best life. A single cowboy with a booty call anytime he wanted." I can practically taste the jealousy on my tongue. "Emily didn't hold anything back on those details."

I can feel his stare on the side of my face. It heats with how I just lashed out. It's not fair and I know it, but I can't help it. Her ugly words still swarm around in my brain like a tiny amoeba.

"Look at me." Maddox's voice is hard, and for a second I'm afraid he's angry with me.

I turn and meet his narrowed eyes.

"What Emily said was out of line. Back then I knew you were aware we had hooked up. I never hid that from you."

I lift a brow. "Yeah, you just flaunted it."

He shoots me a pointed look. "I honestly can't even remember the last time I spent time with her."

"Maddox, I'm not angry. I understand you had needs..."

"My needs were met with my right hand and have been since the day you left this ranch. Until the night I slid inside of you again."

My jaw drops. He what?

I laugh nervously. "What are you saying?"

He tucks a piece of hair behind my ear. "What I'm saying is not one woman has warmed my bed since that night in the barn."

I stare, stunned. "You can't be serious."

"Deadly. Now put away any of that old shit and come here and kiss me," he demands.

Smiling, I lean forward, pressing a kiss to my favorite pair of lips. He begins to deepen it when my phone buzzes on the table next to me.

My heart drops to my stomach when I read the text.

Cooper: Family meeting at Penelope's. Now.

Chapter Fifty-Seven

Maddox

I hold Ivy's hand as we sit in Penelope's living room. Ruthie smirks, but Emmett stares at our clasped hands before he rubs his forehead. Cooper is propped up against the kitchen counter, a casserole dish in one hand and a fork in the other. Ryder is at the dining table. His dirty cowboy hat resting in the middle while he fiddles with his pocketknife.

"Anyone like any tea?" Penelope calls out.

"I'll take one," Cooper calls over his shoulder.

Ivy squeezes my hand, and I smooth my thumb over her knuckles.

"Can someone please let me in on what's happening?" She asks.

Emmett reaches for Ruthie's hand and smiles. "Sam called with some news."

"What news?" She scoots forward on the couch, her full attention on her father.

"Warren made a confession," Ruthie inserts.

"Confession?" Cooper questions.

Emmett shakes his head in disbelief. "Warren Nixon confessed to accepting a bribe from Rocky Bernard to falsify the report. Rule it as an arson so we couldn't collect the insurance money and be forced to sell."

"Holy shit," Cooper blanches.

"Language," Penelope scolds, popping him with a dish rag.

"I'm so confused." Ivy lets go of my hand to place her fingers at her temples. "He just decided to make a confession out of nowhere?"

I glance over at Ryder who still holds an emotionless expression. I'm smiling inside as I scan over his knuckles again. The battered skin is telling.

"Maybe he had a change of heart." Ryder shrugs. "Maybe some self-reflection had his eyes opening."

We all stare at him, well aware he played a part, but no one daring enough to ask the details.

"So, what now?" Ivy questions.

"Now we make our claim. Get the insurance pay out and save our ranch. Warren admitted it was an electrical problem in the attic that caused the fire."

Ivy leans her head back, relief flashing over her face.

"I told you," I whisper. I tilt my chin at Emmett. "I'm sorry for what you lost. But I'm glad you can rebuild even better than before."

"I owe you a big thanks. You pulled me from those flames. Saved my life." He glances at our hands again. "With that being said, I guess I need to address the elephant in the room. Are you dating my daughter?"

I chuckle and nod my head. "Yes sir."

He points at Ivy. "Please don't run him off. He's a hell of a bucking bull breeder."

Ivy rolls her eyes. "Don't worry, dad. I think I'll keep this one."

Running my hand over her back, she smiles at me, and it's the first time since she's been here, I see complete joy on her face.

Chapter Fifty-Eight

Ivy

"So, you and Maddox, huh?" Mom snickers as she places a shirt on a wire hanger.

I'm helping her hang clothes while Dad, Cooper, Ryder, and Maddox play cards in the dining room.

"I mean, I've always thought he was the hotter brother."

"Mom!" I gasp.

"What? I'm not blind, sweetheart," she teases. "So, what's going on? Does this mean you are staying?" Her blue eyes look hopeful, and I sit down on the edge of the bed.

"I would like to. I still have an apartment to deal with and I have a job." I sigh. "It may take me a bit, but I would like to come home."

She places a hand on her heart. "I would love that."

"Mom...about what happened. With dad." I shift on the bed. "I'm so sorry."

Her hand cups my jaw. "You have nothing to be sorry for."

"Why did you forgive him?" I ask.

I spent a long time trying to put myself in her shoes. Would I have forgiven Maddox?

She places a hanger down on the bed. "Marriage is hard. Loving a cowboy even harder. There's a lot of things we do to protect each other. To protect our children. And I owe everything to your father. He saved my life once upon a time and I had a choice to make. I can assure you it wasn't made lightly. But I chose forgiveness. I chose to fight for the love I wanted."

Her answer has a smile forming on my lips. "I'm glad you did."

She smiles. "Me too. Now can you grab that other box of hangers from the floor over there."

"Sure." I slip off the bed and walk to the other side.

Crouching down, I reach for the box, but a photograph on the floor snags my attention.

I pick up the baby photo I recognize then see another fall down in its place. I lift the bed skirt and slide out the box overflowing with old photographs. My baby pictures. Cooper's and Ryder's as well, mixed in with mom and dad's wedding photos. I frown when I spot the small white folder that's always held our birth certificates. Confusion clouds my brain as I vividly remember this exact box in our attic next to grandma's trunk.

"Mom," I croak. I stand, holding the box in my hand. "Why do you have these?"

These should have been destroyed in the fire. Everything was destroyed.

Her face draws down, the story she was telling fading as she sees what I'm holding.

"Mom," I press.

She calmly holds a finger to her lips. "Keep your voice down, Ivy."

I look at the pictures, then back up to her.

"It was you?"

She straightens her shoulders, a mother's strength in her stance. "I told you. I chose to fight."

Ruthie

Eight days ago

Sweat drips from my brow as I finish stripping the last wire. I swipe my forehead before I stand, my hand gripping my lower back. Three days ago, I was digging for paperwork regarding our health insurance when I came across the stacks of past due notices Emmett had tried but failed to hide. It wasn't hard to see what the red stamped notices meant, and the fifty-thousand-dollar tax bill is what hammered in just how much trouble this ranch was in. I kept quiet. Kept in the kitchen, cooking food and raising babies. I left the finances to Emmett, but it's clear he's spiraling. Along with the ranch. After combing through what documents, I could get my hands on. I knew what our options were. Sell or, lose it. And neither was an option. I had a duty. A family. A husband. And I would protect him with every fiber of my being. Even if that meant burning down his ranch, to save it.

Epilogue

Ivy

Four months later

"Ladies and gentlemen, let's give a round of applause for your local stock contractors who made this event here in your hometown of Mayson Ridge, Texas possible."

Cheers echo around the arena as Maddox and my father wave from the middle. Mayson Ridge Ranch is alive and well, and in the process of rebuilding stronger than ever. Unfortunately, even after Warren provided proof of Rocky's bribe, he was able to pay his way out of criminal charges. He's still flaunting around town, acting as if he didn't try to set my family up for failure. It was a miracle Warren even confessed, and since that day in the back bedroom with my mother, I've never shared the truth. Not even with Maddox.

Maddox smiles, his body looking illegal in his starched jeans and button-down shirt. His cowboy hat makes my heart flutter, and I down right swoon when he throws me a wink when I scream loud, whooping and hollering for my man who happens to be on his way to being one of the most well known stock contractors around.

We had to spend almost a month apart when I went back to Georgia to pack up my things and try to convince Merit to move to Texas. She declined but promised to come visit if she ever got the chance.

"You know, Ivy. Your dad is kind of hot." Dakota squints her eyes. "He kind of has that Sam Elliot vibe going."

I glance at Laiken who laughs.

"Please tell me you don't have a crush on my dad too," I deadpan.

She shrugs. "I have to agree with her on this one."

Dakota fist pumps when the announcer booms that the bull riding is almost underway.

"Letttsss gooo!" This comes from Trace as he shouts from his place on Cooper's shoulders. "Parker Stillwater will be here tonight." He beams. "He's my main man." He kicks his boot covered feet in excitement. "He can ride the shit out of a bull."

"Trace!" Laiken shrieks before planting a palm to her forehead.

I laugh, wrapping her in a hug as she tries to hide her smile.

"The boy has spirit," I tell her.

"Yeah. Too much sometimes." She rolls her eyes. "I mean seriously. He can't like any other bull rider besides Parker?"

I side eye her. "What's the beef with you and my cousin anyway? You've known him for years."

"Exactly," she deadpans before Trace is calling her name.

The announcer jabbers something else, but I can't quite understand him over the loud cheers. Murmurs spread out over the crowd before Dakota is nudging me in the arm.

"What?" I face her.

"I think you are being summoned." She points.

My stomach flips upside down when I see Maddox in the arena, waving me to him. Scurrying through the crowd, I climb the white pipe fence in my favorite sundress before I'm tracking across the dirt to my favorite person in the entire world. Maddox had been telling me he wanted to marry me for the last two months. Every night when we go to bed, he shows me just how much he loves me. He whispers in my ear how he can't wait to call me his *wife*. My cheeks flame just thinking about it as I walk up to the man that I never really thought would be mine.

"Hi," I smile.

"Hey, baby." He leans in pressing a kiss to my forehead.

"Is this why you wanted me to wear this dress?" I question.

He grins. "It's my favorite. For a lot reasons." His face heats as he takes me in.

The crowd screams and he captures my hand in his. "I have a question, and I thought the only proper way to ask was to do it when I know we're being televised so the entire world knows whose wife you're going to be."

Tears fill my eyes as he drops to a knee in the dirty arena. "I love you, Ivy Mayson. And I won't take no for an answer. Marry me."

A sob breaks from my chest as he slides the solitaire diamond on my finger. "Yes," I choke out. "Yes."

He wraps me up, spinning me around as he whispers over and over how much he loves me.

After a successful night and a few too many drinks to celebrate the engagement along with Parker winning the entire event, we pull up in Cooper's truck to the big house that's still under construction.

I climb out, followed by Maddox who immediately wraps an arm around my waist and pulls my back to his chest. Dakota jumps from the front seat and slams the door as she belts out a horrific version of a Laney Wilson song.

"Woah!" Cooper hollers, causing us to break apart and bolt in his direction. "Who the hell are you?" He growls.

My boots carry me around the hood of his truck to see a figure standing on the steps of the house. The tiny human moves with confidence, stepping into the light that's being cast by mostly the moon. A teenage girl, no older than thirteen with long dark hair stands before us, planting her hands on her hips as she blows a pink bubble.

"I'm looking for Dakota Sterling," she says after popping the blob of gum and tucking it back into her mouth.

"I'm Dakota Sterling." Dakota idles up to the girl, her body language alert.

The girl hikes her backpack up onto her shoulder. "Sweet. I'm Arizona Sterling. Mind if I crash?"

Dakota frowns. "Who are you?"

The teen crosses her arms with a smirk. "I figured she never told you." She rolls her eyes. "Surprise. I'm your little sister."

The end.

Thank You

Thank you for reading ***Every Single Wildflower***, book one of the ***Every Single Series***.

Curious about the golden retriever cowboy and his wild card best friend?

Cooper and Dakota's story is coming soon!

A fake marriage, friends to lovers, cowboy romance!

For other books or information on release dates and all things S .J. Chaynie, visit **www.authorsjchaynie.com** to sign up for my newsletter or follow me on social media.

My Tribe

I have had this book idea on the sidelines for a while now, and I am so glad I finally jumped headfirst into my cowboy era! I married my very own cowboy fifteen years ago, so this story was so familiar, yet exciting to write! Being from Texas, it was refreshing to dig into my small-town roots and bring you this group of characters. So many things in this book are intertwined with my experiences, my hometown, and the Texas lifestyle in general. I want to thank you, readers, for taking the time to dive into my fictional world and for all the support you give by simply turning the pages. Thank you to A. Bone. My partner in plotting. The one to tell me to trash it or write it. You're the best and your support is never unnoticed. Thank you to my beta readers, my arc readers, and everyone who plays a role in brining my books to life. I couldn't do any of this without you. And last but not least, my family. My husband and my girls. You are my heart. Thank you.

About the author

S.J. Chaynie is a small-town Texas girl who has found a love for writing. She enjoys writing romance, with a sprinkle of suspense, and a little humor. If she is not busy writing her newest ideas, she is spending time with her husband and two beautiful daughters. She believes a good book and a lot of laughs is the best medicine. She brings suspense, love, angst, and sometimes the occasional heartbreak to her stories. Always a HEA, but every character and story she holds close to her heart and hopes they touch yours as well.

Printed in Great Britain
by Amazon

59998950R00163

Printed in Great Britain
by Amazon

15321412R00103